The Dragon House

The Dragon House

Darrell Schweitzer

[signed] Darrell Schweitzer

WILDSIDE PRESS

Copryight © 2018 by Darrell Schweitzer.

Published by Wildside Press LLC.
www.wildsidebooks.com

Chapter One
Concerning Edward Longstretch

The driveway wound at least a mile through the dark woods, off the paved road. It might as well have dropped off the edge of the Earth. Once the woods had closed around them that night, their SUV bumped and swayed through a black tunnel that went on forever, with branches thwacking and scraping against the windows and sides. But then they came to a clearing, made a short circuit of a pebble driveway, and lurched to a stop in front of the unlighted house.

"Oh my God! It's a *castle*!" Margaret said.

Nevertheless, it was Edward who first noticed what was genuinely strange about the place.

* * * *

First, particularly in the story of his own life, the basic facts: there was a boy, aged thirteen, named Edward Eusebius Longstretch, which he knew was an awful name, or at least part of it was. He didn't even mind the Eusebius, which he simply didn't use, but it didn't help that there had once been a Philadelphia politician named Thatcher Longst*reth*, which only sounded like a lisping version of his, something he'd had sputtered into his face at school any number of times.

That meant that he had to be very careful with the only serviceable part of his name, which was Edward, never Ed, Eddie, or even, as some people weirdly attempted it, Ted. Just Edward. His sister Margaret was two years older than him, and maybe she didn't care—maybe girls just *didn't*—and her name could easily fold up like origami into Marge, Maggie, or even Mags, but he refused to answer to anything but Edward.

Edward never quite fit in anywhere, even in his own family. For one thing, he was short, thin, and olive-skinned, with black, straight hair and dark eyes, while both of his parents were towering, massive

THE DRAGON HOUSE | 5

people with curly, ginger hair—his father's voluminous muttonchops going somewhat white, his hairline receding—and as for Edward's sister, he could well imagine her singing the lead in a Wagnerian opera. He was precocious enough to know what a Wagnerian opera was, and he'd often giggled himself to sleep at the thought of Margaret in a winged helmet and cast-iron corset, spear in hand, bellowing out "Die Valkyrie," only with Elmer Fudd lyrics: "Kill da wabbit! Kill da WABBIT!"

He himself was sometimes asked in all seriousness, or else as a tease, whether he was an Indian, that is, a Native American, and he would reply in an entirely deadpan way that he was a member of the Runnamuk tribe and inclined to take scalps and he didn't care how politically incorrect that sounded.

His father, who was also named Edward but was called Ed by Mom to avoid confusion—none of this "Big Edward" and "Little Edward" or "Junior" stuff, which *Edward* would never have tolerated—was in addition to his hugeness, a decidedly mysterious person, who sometimes said he was a scientist and sometimes said he was a salesman and sometimes a journalist, and went away on long trips and sometimes brought back for Edward strange coins with square holes in them, or mounted specimens of iridescent blue butterflies, or dinosaur bones or million year old shark's teeth three inches long and still sharp. Sometimes Edward thought his father was a spy, and once he had confided in a kid he thought was his friend that his dad worked for the CIA and was a double-zero agent just like James Bond; but when *that* got around the school it was considerably worse than having a sputter at the end of your name and had brought him a stern lecture from a teacher about telling lies.

What he'd actually learned was the need to keep secrets, because if his father really was a spy, it wouldn't do to go around telling people about it.

So it was that at the end of the school year, his father had suddenly announced that because of changes in his "business," the whole family was going to move from Philadelphia to someplace far up in the northern and central part of the state, near the New York line, not the Poconos or any such resort area, but one of what Margaret called "flyover places" which are more or less blank on the map and you never pay any attention to them as you fly over them on your way to someplace real.

Margaret was more upset than Edward. Maybe she had more to lose. Edward, at most, mixed feelings leaving his school and his neighborhood. He had a few friends, but not close ones. Probably he wouldn't ever see them again. What he really didn't like was starting all over *yet again*. He was only finishing the eighth grade and this had already happened *twice* in his life, once when he was in the second grade and once when he was in the fifth. He felt like a plant, uprooted and shoved into a new pot. Not a flower. No boy thinks of himself as a flower. Maybe something prickly, with thorns, but uprooted all the same. If Margaret felt uprooted too, well, he had that in common with her. Two pots, side by side on some new ledge somewhere.

So he patiently packed his books and his model airplanes and his mysterious green coins, his "specimens," animal, plant, insect, and mineral. He somewhat less carefully stuffed most of his clothes into a duffel bag, and let the movers do the rest.

On the actual day of the move, the family drove for what seemed like hours, up through the Lehigh Valley tunnel, where, on the other side, the world suddenly opened out into a sweeping vista of green valleys, and hills, and there was a strange formation along a ridgeline that Mom had said was the last vestige of the Great Wall of China and Father had said was built by trolls.

If they'd gone on, they would have ended up in the Poconos, which is where richer or more normal families than theirs went for skiing or boating or whatever; but after a while they took an unfamiliar exit and made their way north and west, past a few farms and barns, then past not much of anything but woods, as the miles went by and the roads grew narrower and rougher and the woods darker.

Margaret got bored as the trip progressed, said less, and settled down to read one of her magazines. Edward, who had been trying to play a videogame that didn't really interest him, put it aside and just stared out the window. As the sun started to set and night seemed to fill the valleys first, where it was entirely dark but for the light of the very occasional farmhouse, it occurred to Edward that out here civilization, the very presence of mankind itself, was only in those valleys. Along the long and sloping ridges there was *nothing*, just trees as they had always been since the beginning of time. Since those ridges and hills connected, one to another, you could probably smuggle a whole, huge army of Orcs down from Canada all the way to Harrisburg as long as they didn't shoot off fireworks or play their boom boxes too loudly, and no one would ever be the wiser.

It was a sinister thought. This was a landscape that could hold secrets.

Then they turned off the paved road, onto the unpaved driveway or Indian path or whatever it was, startling several deer out of the way with the headlights, and they came to the house, and Margaret made her celebrated remark about it being a castle.

Edward wondered what a castle was doing here, but said nothing.

"Well, it certainly is big, isn't it Ed?" Mom said.

"It'll do," Dad replied. "Let me go in first and see if I can find the lights."

The rest of them got out on the driveway and stared up at the house—which was indeed huge—with more gables and turrets and high windows and strange turnings of the roof than the eye could take in all at once. The full moon had risen. Moonlight gleamed off some of the high windows, and it seemed to Edward that the windows had odd shapes, not rectangular or square or even round, but some of them, curved into a larger Gothic arch, looked like the outlines of *bats* with their wings outspread and there might even have been one that wound around the side of the tower like a wriggling snake made of many colors of glass panes.

But what Edward noticed first, when his father inevitably found the electrical system and turned on the lights, was that high up, above several layers of roof and a balcony or two, there were two windows that bulged out like domes on an observatory, and these, when lit, gave the impression of *eyes*.

Lit up, in the dark, the house looked to be *alive,* something slowly stirring awake, and aware that they were about to go inside.

Suddenly he felt very cold, and shivered, rubbing his arms.

"Ooh!" said Margaret behind him, skittering her fingers across his neck like a spider. "I bet it's *haunted!*"

"Quit it!" Edward said and stepped away from her.

He really *was* cold. In the city, that morning, it had been sweltering, so he was wearing shorts and a tank-top and flip-flop sandals, which were not at all appropriate here. He looked out into the dark woods and decided that this was probably buckskin-and-moccasin country, but, lacking those, he'd have to change into long jeans and a sweatshirt. He'd need a good pair of hiking boots if he wanted to do any exploring.

So he was *cold*. He wasn't *afraid*. He didn't regard the house with *dread*, or *trepidation* or even what you could call *unease*. It was more a sense of waiting to see what was going to happen next, like when you meet a strange dog on a path in the park and you look at it and it looks at you and both of you are waiting for the other to make the first move.

Of course the house was a lot bigger than a dog, and he knew that houses are made of wood and stone and not really alive, but still he wondered what this one *thought* of him.

If he shivered, he told himself yet again, it was because he was underdressed for a night like this. Nothing more.

Everyone else had already gone inside. He stood there, looking up, shivering.

"Edward?" his father called from the open door. "Are you coming?"

"Yes, Dad."

"Hurry up. You'll like this. It's *neat.*"

Edward's father was always using expressions like that. Edward tried not to.

Then some kind of bug bit him on the leg. He grabbed his duffel bag and the box of his specimens out of the back of the car and hurried inside after the rest of the family.

His first impression, stepping in off the porch, was of a high, narrow hall and a staircase leading up from it, and rooms piled high with boxes on either side. It was anything but *neat* in most senses of the word. It was the kind of place that needed a hulking, half-human butler to answer the door and intone in a positively sepulchral voice, *"Whom* shall I say is calling?" and "I will see if the *Master* is in."

Having such a butler would have been, admittedly, neat. But there was no one else there, not even his father, who had gone in without waiting for him.

Dad had said something about how the people from the Agency had come and gone and done their work. Not the movers. The Agency.

Somehow Edward didn't think it was a used-car business.

THE DRAGON HOUSE | 9

He stared up at some of the wooden trimming that went around the top of the walls, up against the ceiling. It was decorated with little bat motifs.

"Edward!" his mother called from somewhere in the back of the house. "Supper in ten minutes!"

He was amazed that his mother could have organized the kitchen that quickly, but his mother was amazing when she put her mind to it.

"I want to go change clothes first," he shouted back. "I'm cold."

"Third floor. Just left of the stairs."

He put one foot on the stairs.

"Don't let the ghosties get you!" his sister shouted from the kitchen.

He hurried up, past a darkened set of rooms piled with boxes and furniture, around a turn in the hall where the lightbulb was out and he couldn't see a thing. His bare shoulder brushed against something that might have been fur or feathers, but smelled old and musty. He didn't pause to investigate, then went up another flight of stars, where, thankfully there was a light on.

The bedroom door was open. He dropped his duffel-bag to the floor in the hallway, then groped his way inside, his specimen box under his left arm. He groped for the light switch and didn't find it. He put the box down on the bed, then went over to the window, which was circular like a porthole, and peered out.

Moonlight gleamed on tiled roofs, their structures so complex that they seemed like the waves on a choppy sea. This place was *big*. He still wanted to know why anyone would go through so much trouble to build a house this large out in the middle of nowhere, and *how* they managed to haul all that building material out here, so far from any main roads, much less *when* it was done. The place was not new. He doubted it was built by modern contractors with cranes and bulldozers.

He looked further, letting his eyes adjust, and he thought he saw something shining beyond the treetops, in the far distance, a lake perhaps.

Nearer at hand, there was something startling. Gargoyles on the rooftops? He looked across to a square tower, which actually had battlements like a castle. There were hunched, winged and clawed shapes perched on all four corners.

And as he watched, one of them leaned forward, dropped into the air, and soared off, flapping slowly. It had to be a bird of some kind, a crow perhaps, but it seemed to have a tail, trailing behind it like the tail of a snake.

He turned back from the window, and brushed something with his leg.

It was his sister's suitcase.

He forgot all about towers and gargoyles. This would have to be settled. This was to be *his* room. He was much too old to share.

He changed into jeans and a sweat shirt and sneakers and hurried downstairs.

* * * *

It was settled, over dinner and later, that the room was to be Edward's, but that Margaret's room, which was at the other end of the hall, wasn't ready yet, either filled with boxes or needing work. So, for the time being Edward and his sister were going to have to "bunk" together, though neither of them liked the idea very much.

After supper, their parents lit a fire in the huge fireplace in the downstairs living room (in a house this size, there had to be more than one "living room," so it was useful to label them early), and Father first did magic tricks, the kind he often did to entertain them, with cards, balls, and magic coins that he suddenly snatched out of someone's ear. Then he told stories, some of his wild stories, about dragons that flew between planets, and fought in the depths of space, and heroes who rode on them, and how the dragons sometimes fell to earth and lay in the ground, sleeping, until the earth covered them over and only very few people knew they were there.

"You know the Face on Mars?" Father said. "That's a dragon."

Edward asked why his father didn't write these stories down and make a book out of them, because it was the sort of book he liked to read, and he knew other kids would like it too, but his father only said, "No, these stories aren't for writing down."

Later, he pulled on the running pants he used as pajamas in cold weather and climbed into bed with his sister. They'd never found the light switch, but in the dark, by moonlight, he could tell that she was wide awake, with her hands folded behind her head, staring up at the ceiling.

"Mags? What is it?"

"I don't like being here."

Edward hadn't actually shared a bed with his sister since he was about five, so he didn't like it either, and he almost said something to that effect, but he sensed that that wasn't what she was getting at.

"I feel like Rapunzel. I hate that."

"I thought you liked fairy tales."

"I do, but I don't want to be *living* in one, you know, a princess locked away in this tower until maybe, just maybe, somebody comes and rescues me before I turn ninety."

"You could start growing your hair really long."

She reached over and yanked his hair, but good-naturedly.

"I will *not* have a fire-escape growing out of my head. Prince Charming is going to have to come up the stairs like anybody else."

"Well there is a town around here somewhere. We'll be going to school there in September."

"So?" she said.

"Well pardon my showing off my brilliant powers of deduction, but that means there will be other kids there, including, well, you know…boys. One of them might be named Prince Charming. You can look in the phonebook under P."

She sighed and locked her hands behind her head again, staring into the darkness above them.

"I bet the boys in this town all go barefoot and wear straw hats and chew tobacco and smell like cows—"

Edward reached over and caught her ankle with his toes.

"*Moo…!*"

She kicked him away. "Oh, shut up and go to sleep!"

Now it was his turn to lie awake for a while, listening to the sounds of the house as it creaked and settled. Maybe he heard something scampering, mice or squirrels in the walls. He expected as much. He tried to sort out his feelings toward his sister. He didn't dislike her. She was just…his sister, always there, a part of his life like the weather. But she was a girl, and girls as a rule didn't make sense, even if, in this instance, he actually *did* understand more or less how she felt. He couldn't focus the thought any better than that.

* * * *

What happened later must have been a dream. He was crawling in the dark, up a tight, narrow staircase. He felt smooth, cold wood beneath his hands and his bare feet. He had on the sweatshirt and running pants he'd worn to bed.

Sometimes the way was so narrow that he had to twist and wriggle to get through, and even in a dream, he could only wonder why anyone would design a back stair or secret passageway like that.

At first the only sound was of his own breathing. He was panting, as if he'd been scrambling up these stairs for some time, for longer than he could remember. Possibly he should be afraid. Possibly he was being chased by someone or some thing, but that was the part of the dream he had already forgotten.

He went on climbing, up, and up, around and around, as the passage grew narrower and narrower, and it came to him that the house itself was *breathing,* the creaking and settling sounds he heard in the distance, branches scraping against windows, shutters flapping in the wind, had a distinct rhythm to them.

The passage was too cramped for him to stand up. He had to grab each step with his hands and crawl.

The wood felt soft somehow, pliable, as if it were alive, like the flesh of an animal.

And the wind and the creaking sounds formed actual words. The house spoke to him.

"Edward."

That was all it said, but in the dream, which was crazy, the house knew he was there and knew his name.

He realized that he was trapped, that if he tried backing down the way he'd come, the stairs would go on forever, as they would above him, and the passage would get narrower and narrower whichever way he went.

Now he *was* afraid and he began to pound on the walls with his fists, and kick, and to scream.

The passage was too narrow. He couldn't turn around. He couldn't even roll onto his side.

Suddenly there was a blaze of light, and he was tumbling forward, and before he knew it he'd fallen out of a closet onto the kitchen floor amid an avalanche of brooms and jars.

"Edward!" said his mother. "How ever did you get *in there?"*

"What's going on?" his father said. His father held a flashlight, which seemed redundant since overhead light was blazing.

"I think he was sleepwalking." his mother said.

"That's not like him," his father said.

He'd been crying. His mother hugged him and wiped his cheeks with her nightgown, and now he was more embarrassed than afraid.

"It's all right, honey," she said.

"Yeah."

She took him by the hand. "I'll take you back up to bed."

He pulled away. "Mom! I'm not a little kid! I can go up by myself."

He went, and when he got there, Margaret was still asleep as if nothing had happened. She stirred as he got back into bed.

"What…? Huh…?"

"Nothing," he whispered. "Just had to go to the bathroom. Go back to sleep."

Chapter Two
Stuff, More Stuff, and Cannons

The next morning, after breakfast, Mom told Edward to help his sister get her room ready. He helped her move a few boxes, and he opened the blinds and gathered up a big, double handful of dust from the windowsill. When she opened the window, he hurled the dustball out, hoping to watch it trail over the rooftops like a snowball, but instead it just dissipated in a single puff.

After that, he wasn't much needed. It was as if the house had begun to put things in order all by itself.

Last night, in the dark, her room had seemed packed solid. Now there was still some mess, but plenty of space to move around.

She took the top cover off her bed and shook that out the window, then put it back on the bed.

He went back to his own room, got her suitcase, and brought it to her.

"Do you want to go exploring?" he said.

"Later. I got more important things to do first."

He left her sitting with her laptop computer on the windowsill, busily telling her friends on My Space about her adventures.

Edward had only one thing *he* needed to do first.

He'd heard someone say—or possibly his father had quoted it to him, as a joke—that *home* is where you keep your *stuff* while you are out getting other *stuff*. While he wasn't actively acquiring more stuff just now, he understood the sentiment.

A couple more boxes of his stuff had arrived in the room that morning. Possibly his father had fetched them from the car while he was helping Margaret.

He got to work.

He left his clothes in the duffel bag for the moment, clearing a shelf in a well-lit part of the room—but out of the direct sun, which was bad for everything from books to dead butterflies—and then carefully arranging what he thought of as his little museum. First, his favorite books, not all that many, only a couple dozen in all, but each of which was something special, an important part of his life: a few picture books, such as *The World of Insects,* and *Dinosaurs,* and books about exploration and going to the Moon, and *The Lord of the Rings* and *The Adventures of Huckleberry Finn* and even one little volume which had gotten him into trouble a few times when he'd tried quoting it to people who thought they were smarter than he was, *Famous Insults.* He also had books on magic and history and famous scientists. There was a box of Japanese manga which he liked, but which weren't as important to him. (These, box and all, he slid under the bed.)

Then came the specimens: The iridescent blue *morpho* butterfly from the Amazon, framed inside a glass mount on a bed of cotton, and a rather rough fossil trilobite (named Trilby) the size of a potato, and a plastic tray with a cover and lots of compartments—the kind a carpenter uses to sort different sizes of nails and screws, but Edward had carefully filled the compartments shark's teeth and shells, and his mysterious green coins with the square holes in them, and tiny toy figures, and he even left one space empty, reserved for an Indian arrowhead, because he was certain that in a place like this, he was going to find an arrowhead.

He had a model of a Fokker Triplane to die for, a masterpiece he and his father had once assembled and painted together at Christmas. This occupied a place of honor on top of the shelves, next to the wind-up tarantula, the metal statue of a wizard holding a real, multifaceted crystal in his hands, and the plastic, three-headed dog.

In other words, *stuff.* Now that he had a place for his stuff, this really was his room, a place he could come back to.

It was time to go exploring.

He looked out the window. It was a clear, bright day, and the woods looked inviting. In the city, there had been a few parks, but getting out into real woods was a rare treat.

But he also listened to the wind blowing and buffeting the endless corners and angles and roofs, and somewhere it must have been blowing over a pipe the way you blow over the mouth of a bottle, making a low, mournful sound, and he decided, no, the house first.

The walls and ceiling creaked just a little, as if in agreement.

On the far side of his room was what he'd taken for a closet, but now that he opened the door, he saw a flight of steps leading up. He paused. He wasn't entirely sure the door had been here last night, but then he told himself that was silly. It had been dark. They hadn't even been able to find the light switch. Of course he didn't notice.

He put one sneakered foot on the first step, and felt nothing in particular. Just wood. He put his hand on the side of the wall, inside the stairway and felt only plaster. Maybe it was a little cold.

So he made his way upward, into semi-darkness, and it occurred to him that maybe he should have brought a flashlight, but he wasn't entirely sure where there was a flashlight just now, and he didn't want to ask Mom or Dad for one, because they might demand to know what he was doing and forbid him to do it.

Better to just go on, and then tell them afterwards about what he'd found.

Just above his own room, he found another bedroom, furnished with a big, ornate mirror and framed pictures of people from very long ago. The cover of the bed was very dusty. Inside the closets hung old, musty-smelling clothes, old-fashioned women's clothes, as if his grandmother's grandmother had lived here once and hadn't come back in a hundred years. There was a nightstand, a makeup table in front of a smaller mirror, and even some old jewelry in a box in the first drawer; but he almost felt that he was intruding, and so hurried on out of this room, along a hallway, and up yet another flight of narrow, rickety stairs, past a whole series of portraits of what looked like somebody's ancestors in various period costumes, only with the faces of frogs, until he came to a high-ceilinged, gloomy, musty loft that was filled with *stuff*.

That was the only way he could express it, even to himself: *stuff*.

It wasn't that most of the stuff was stuffed—it wasn't, save for the two polar bears, standing upright, one wearing a gentleman's tuxedo jacket and top hat, the other draped in pearls, the two of them positioned as if dancing a waltz.

Part of the room might have once been a nursery, which was a word he'd learned from old books and really meant a playroom. There were very old-fashioned toys all about, tin soldiers, a rocking horse, a Noah's Ark with carved animals.

Edward was just old enough to feel self-conscious about playing with toys, but when he squeezed between an ancient tricycle with an enormous front wheel and several mummy cases, and beheld the almost endless electric train layout, which stretched out into the gloom farther than he could see, he just gave up any resistance, let out an involuntary "wow." He spent quite a long time admiring the many levels of tracks that wound through tunnels and between mountains covered with forests of tiny trees. There were lakes and towns and even, on one of the mountains, a vast mish-mash of a house that he was certain represented the one he was in right now.

He saw a few cars on sidings, but began looking for the train. Then he found the control switches, and turned the metal lever just a little bit to the right. Something rumbled. He turned it a little more, and the whole layout seemed to come to life, tiny lights going in the windows of the houses, figures moving through the streets, even, on a painted lawn close by, a tiny boy throwing a stick smaller than a toothpick for a mechanical dog to fetch.

When the train itself came roaring out of the tunnel beneath the papier mache mountains, headlight gleaming, a steam engine puffing real smoke, he forgot about everything else.

A steam engine, of course.

Somehow electric trains seem better with steam engines, Edward realized, though he wasn't old enough to have ever seen a real one outside of a museum.

And this was no ordinary steam engine. It was more than magnificent. It had a face, and, he saw now, twin headlights like eyes. It was scaled on the side like a dragon, with streaming fins and whiskers, and it hauled car after car, more than he could look at very closely, but the impression he had—maybe it was a trick of the motion—was that the people and things on that train were alive. In one ornate car with banners flying, a Chinese emperor sat on his throne while silk-robed ambassadors bowed before him and presented gifts; in another there was a ballroom, and people were dancing; in yet another something like a sea-serpent swam around and around in a tiny tank of water; in yet another, lightning bolts crackled; in one more, completely incongruous medieval knights and ladies sat primly in the seats; from another, hordes of animate skeletons wriggled and clambered out the windows and onto the roof; and in several more there was only darkness, not as if the windows were blacked out, but more as if there were, truly *nothing* inside, not an empty car, but an active, light-devouring nothing that could swallow up the whole world if it ever got loose.

Around and around the train raced, disappearing and appearing again on different levels, over bridges, among treetops, above the mountains on more mountains he hadn't been able to see before, and finally, as his eyes completely adjusted to the gloom, he saw the train spiral in darkness among tiny motes of light that looked like stars, and then vanish into the ceiling far above, dragging the stars after it as if it had sucked them into a vacuum cleaner.

Edward could only stare up in amazement for several minutes. Then it occurred to him to wonder where the train went.

This time be didn't find a stairway, but a rope ladder that hung from the ceiling, and he climbed it, higher than he expected to, as if somehow he'd hugely misjudged the distance or if—Impossible? Well, maybe not—the house just kept growing as he ascended.

But eventually his head bumped into a trap door and he pushed up into an even gloomier attic room where huge and mysterious machines ground and clanked and whined. He got out of there as quickly as he could and found himself in a circular room where the floor turned, like an enormous carousel, only the animals were all monsters of various sorts, spiked, with claws and scales, not anything he cared to sit on. He tried to walk, from post to post, while the room turned and he got thoroughly dizzy, and it was more by chance that he managed to stumble off the carousel and through a door.

He landed sprawling in yet another, semi-darkened room. He just sat there, on a not-very clean carpet, his head spinning.

"And so Edward, have you seen everything?"

He looked up blearily. *"Dad?"*

His father helped him to his feet. Edward stood there, unsteadily. Dad was wearing what looked like a sea captain's uniform, with lots of brass buttons.

"I knew you were coming, Edward. It was quite inevitable."

"Dad—? I don't understand a lot of things."

Dad put his hand on Edward's shoulder and walked with him over to a somewhat brighter part of the room, where late afternoon sunlight (was it late afternoon already?) streamed through a tall window between massive bookcases.

Edward realized that he was in a library, which like so much in this house, seemed to go on and on forever.

"There are a lot of things, Son, that no one entirely understands."

"Like this house?"

"Perhaps. You could say that."

"I just *did* say that," said Edward.

"Indeed. Verily. There are mysteries upon mysteries…"

"Like, why did we move here?"

"…not all of which you are ready to understand yet, though that understanding will come in time."

Edward tried to keep calm and be patient, but he hated it when his father went into fortune-cookie mode and talked like this. He wanted more direct answers.

"Like, *whose* stuff *is* all this and how *did* it get here?"

"Ah yes," said his father. "Whose? How? Why? How much? Well to answer one question, it has just accumulated. For another—I don't suppose you got to see it *all*, not everything—?"

"I don't think so."

"—not the blue whale, the full-sized plaster replica of the Great Pyramid of Cheops that the Victoria and Albert Museum in London rejected because they couldn't fit it through the front door, the tap-dancing mechanical tyrannosaurs, the original score of the song the Sirens sang in the handwriting of the goddess Venus, the Martian village, the wreck of the *Titanic*—the real one, not that fake thing on the bottom of the Atlantic—"

"Dad!"

"It's a shame. It's a great collection. Really worth an extended visit."

"Dad!" Edward stamped his foot, hard. All this was too much, just *too much*.

But his father just grabbed him by the arm and led him back through the stacks of the great library. Edward looked up. The shelves rose, tier upon tier, balcony upon balcony, perhaps forever. Somewhere, high above, something fluttered, a bat or a bird. A ball of dust, like the one he'd thrown out of his sister's window, landed at his feet with a soft whisper of sound. He had to look away, sneezing, and wiped his eyes.

"Dad…?"

"It's all here, Edward. The collective brain of the house. There is almost limitless knowledge stored in this room. An infinity of answers, if only you know how to ask the right question. Some of this, I tell you in all seriousness, you are going to need in the future. This is your education—"

"I thought I was going to school somewhere in September—"

"—some of which no one has ever mastered. Look here."

His father took down a volume from a shelf marked "tomes" and placed it on a table. Edward decided that a tome was like an ordinary book, only thicker and more sloppily bound. This one was in very beat-up leather, with the covers almost falling off. At first it didn't seem to have a title, but Father just set it down on a table in a beam of sunlight and let Edward stare at it for a moment.

Then the title seemed to be, *The Book of Unmaking*.

"Go ahead, open it."

He lifted the heavy cover. On the first page was a scene of a marvelous city, all green stone and swirly spires, with vehicles like mechanical birds soaring between the towers. But even as he looked on it, the page faded to blank.

"Too bad," said his father. "I'd wanted to visit there."

Edward turned another page, on which were depicted in vivid colors and stunning detail numerous brightly colored butterflies and moths, all species he'd never seen, even an iridescent blue, long-tailed thing that looked like an impossible version of the familiar, green luna moth.

They faded away.

Father made a *tsk-tsk* sound. "Extinct, alas."

Edward didn't turn the next page.

Father turned the book over on the tabletop with a thud. He opened what should have been the back cover, but it didn't seem to be. This was a new book, and its title, beautifully lettered in brilliant blues and golds, was *The Book of Making*.

"Go ahead."

Edward turned the page and saw, at first, nothing, but then a picture slowly appeared, of a field of brilliant orange grass, and tall creatures like nothing he'd ever seen before grazing there—he thought of a cross between a giraffe and a snail, but that wasn't right. The whole scene wasn't right. There were three suns in the sky.

He turned another page and saw a machine that looked like an enormous alarm clock with wings, soaring through clouds. From the underside hung a basket, in which a man and a woman in old-fashioned clothes (he in a top-hat, she in a frilly bonnet) comfortably sipped champagne from tall-stemmed glasses.

"You get the idea," said Edward's father.

"Not really—"

"In time, in time."

Now they turned to another bookcase, which had iron bars over the front. Rattling keys, his father opened it. Even so, the books were chained to the shelves.

"This is the dark stuff," his father said. "Oh, we have whole rooms of Forgotten Lore—or we did, except I'm not sure where it is—not to mention Nameless lore—difficult to find anything there, because none of the books have titles—but this, *this* is the real *creme de la creeps*—the nightmare knowledge—but even this may save you someday, if you use it wisely, or destroy you, if you don't."

"Save me from *what?*"

"Don't even open them yet. Just look at the titles. All you need to know is that they're here."

So Edward looked and saw Fabius Magister's *Ye Booke of Goinge Unto Ye Darke Worldes* and Professor Hieronymous Frightfest's *Really Scary Secrets* in two volumes, not to mention Arlo Freebdian's *Ghastly Horrors and What To Do About Them*, next to *Spilchfarb and Other Appalling Revelations from the Book of Gibberish* by L. Allan Weinstein, the *Cultes des Ghoules* by the Comte D'Erlette, the *Book of Eibon, Unausprechlichen Kulten,* and a dog-eared paperback of the dread *Necronomicon* of Abdul Alhazred, guaranteed to drive readers insane or your money back, after which they would inevitably turn to *The Book of the Mad* and *The Book of the Madder* and then perhaps cross-reference the somewhat thinner *Book of the Somewhat Irate*, which was in turn stuffed in tightly between the 2006 edition of Fodor's *Yuggoth* and *The Plateau of Leng on Five Dollars a Day.*

Edward felt his head spinning. All of this was entirely too crazy for words. Just to think that two days ago he had been living in a rowhouse in Philadelphia. He almost felt like giving up, just opening the *Necronomicon* at random and screaming the text aloud in pig-latin.

He considered several possible explanations: that *all* of this was a dream and he would wake up in the morning in his old room in that very same rowhouse; that he *was* going insane without even bothering to read the *Necronomicon*; that he had been abducted by aliens and they were messing with his mind and implanting screen memories so he'd *think* he was going insane; or that his father was entirely and completely stark, raving bonkers; or—

"Dad," he asked softly. "Are you a magician?"

"Ah," said his father. "The inevitable, sensible, entirely logical question. Am I, *ipso facto, quondam est demonstratum,* a *sorcerer,* a *mage,* a modern Merlin, who will guide the latter-day hidden hero in his rise to greatness?—But I am getting ahead of myself. The answer in short, in one word, is 'No.' I just work here."

"Here?"

"Sort of a caretaker, the latest in a long line of caretakers. But come, Edward, there is one more thing you have to see before you can begin to understand."

His father led him out of the room. He swung open two doors, huge and curving like cathedral doors, and when they stepped out, Edward could only gape and whisper, "Wow," and he had to stop himself before he lapsed into "Gosh," or, worse yet, "Jeepers."

Because he knew where he was. He stood on a polished floor in front of a railing, looking out through two rounded, glass domes, which were, now that he saw them up close, multi-faceted like insect eyes. This room was lit, not with electricity, but with flickering candles that came on all by themselves when Edward and his father entered.

Strangest of all, right by the railing in the center of floor was an enormous steering wheel, like you'd expect to find on the bridge of an ocean liner.

Edward's father took hold of this wheel and turned it very gently, *steering*. The house creaked and shifted beneath Edward's feet. He heard a few books falling in the library, and looked back just in time to see a glowing crystal skull roll off a high shelf to land harmlessly in a box of styrofoam peanuts.

Then he looked out the windows, and saw, not the roof of the house and trees beyond, as he expected, but glowing golden clouds beneath a full moon. The clouds broke against the domes of the windows. The whole house seemed to be racing as if through a golden ocean.

Just then his father reminded him of Captain Nemo in *20,000 Leagues Under the Sea*, and it was disquieting to remember that Captain Nemo was not entirely right in the head.

"Here Edward, you try it."

His father directed him to take the wheel, and closed his hands over Edward's.

"Hold it tight, Son. Let it feel you. You have to *touch*."

That was when Edward noticed that his father was wearing gloves. But he didn't have a chance to say anything, because suddenly he felt a whole flood of sensations, tingling first, then warmth, and then it seemed that he was holding on, not to the handles of a wooden steering wheel, but onto a *living* thing, and then his fingers seemed to sink into the wood, and the wheel gripped him as hard as he gripped it.

He was afraid then, but he didn't struggle. He turned the wheel ever so slightly, when instinct told him to, and he could feel the twistings and turnings of the house itself, the wood creaking and settling.

The clouds streamed away to either side, as if the house were soaring through them and parting them.

"That's good," his father said. "Very good. You must become *one*."

There was Dad in his fortune-cookie mode again, mysterious and vague. Edward remembered the joke about the Zen Buddhist who says to the hot-dog vendor, "Make me one with everything."

But aren't Buddhists vegetarians?

The house lurched and a few more books fell in the library.

"Concentrate," his father said. "If this were a car, I'd remind you to always keep your eyes on the road."

"But it's not, is it?"

"No, it's not, Son."

Edward felt every tremor and creaking of the house now. The house lurched even more and there were several loud crashes as Edward started to pull away, but Father put both of his huge hands on Edward's shoulders and whispered, "Steady. Steady."

And it seemed that Edward was flying, not in his own body. He had become something huge, awesomely powerful, and he felt the surge of great wings, and of an immense body turning and twisting, something that was him and wasn't at the same time.

"Yes," his father said. "This is as it should be. This is what must be."

Edward felt the wind against his face and roaring past his ears, even though he was indoors and there was no wind where he stood.

All his senses were heightened. He could see for hundreds of miles, out, out, over the golden clouds. He saw something out there, moving, a dark shape that rose above the clouds, spread its bat-like wings, and sank down again.

"Dad?"

"Yes, Edward?"

"Are there pterodactyls in this part of Pennsylvania?"

"I don't think so, Edward."

"Dad?"

"Yes?"

"Is that still Pennsylvania out there?"

His father didn't answer that, but instead closed his gloved hands over Edward's wrists, and pulled him away from the steering wheel.

Then Edward was just standing with his father towering over him, looking out through the two observatory windows. He saw rooftops below, and trees, and the family's SUV parked in the driveway.

"Dad?"

"Edward, I think you and I need to keep this between ourselves for the time being. Promise?"

"Promise," Edward said weakly.

"GREAT!" Suddenly his Father was madly energetic, as he sometimes got, and was dragging him along the railing until they came to a wrought-iron spiral staircase. Edward found himself shooed down as quickly as he could go "I promised you something really neat," his father said. "How about THIS?"

"Cannons...?"

They had come to a lower level, at the base of the observatory windows, where there were indeed four cannons, like those on an old-fashioned sailing ship, shoved through gunports and pointing out over the driveway.

"Cannons?" Edward said again.

His father slapped him on the shoulder, hard enough to send Edward staggering. "Yes. Think about it. How many kids do you know who have their own cannons in their house?"

"Not many, Dad." Most of the kids he knew lived in row houses in Philadelphia.

"I should think *not!* Now look. Here's something even *neater!*"

With a heave, his father hauled one of the cannons back from the gunport, into the room. It seemed to move with surprisingly ease, as if the wheels were very well greased, or there was some trick with ball-bearings.

Edward stepped back quickly, afraid the thing would run over his feet.

"Watch this!" his father said, and proceeded to load the cannon, first taking what looked like part of an old bedsheet, then ramming it down the barrel with a ramrod. "Wadding. You've got to have wadding." Then he took something like an enormous flour scoop like Mom had in the kitchen and scooped up a great load of gunpowder out of an open bucket. "Just the right amount. One measure." Then he took a cannonball out of a chute in the wall, and as he did another rolled into its place, the way balls appear one after another in a bowling alley.

He put the ball in the barrel and rammed it into place, followed by a bit more wadding.

"It's *ready,* Edward."

"Uh, ready for what?"

"For *you* to do the rest, Edward."

"Huh?"

"ARGH! Put yer back into it ye lubber! Argh! Argh! Heave to! Heave to! Guns in position!"

Edward was so started that he actually placed both hands on the back of the cannon and pushed with all his strength, while his several previous explanations and a couple of new ones raced through his mind: his father as Captain Nemo, more than a little mad; he himself going mad; this all a crazy dream; or maybe he'd somehow slipped through a portal into an alternate universe—the attic seemed to contain everything *else*, so why not?—and landed himself in a pirate movie.

Much to his amazement, the cannon, which must have weighed a couple tons, actually started to inch forward. Greased wheels. That had to be it. He pushed as hard as he could, gasping and straining, and slowly the cannon rolled into place with a thunk. There was a little groove at the edge of the floor to hold the front two wheels in place.

He paused for a moment, trying to catch his breath.

He smelled something burning.

"Edward..."

He turned and saw that his father was holding in one hand a wooden stick from which a piece of string dangled. In the other he had a cigarette lighter. The string was smoldering, like a fuse.

Father grinned hugely, as if this were the *really neat* surprise he'd been saving.

"Your turn, Edward. You get to do it." He handed Edward the stick, and when Edward hesitated he said, "You see that hole at the end of the cannon? Don't you know anything about gunnery, lad? Argh." This last "argh" carried somewhat less conviction than the previous ones.

Edward went to touch the burning fuse to the hole, when he suddenly felt himself yanked aside.

"Not *behind* it! Off to the *side!* Are you crazy?"

Before Edward could answer or even consider the further possibilities of who might be crazy here, the fuse somehow found its way into the hole, and the cannon went off with a tremendous roar. It leapt back, the wheels flying out of the grooves in the floor and the cannon rolled halfway across the room. Edward looked after it realizing that he could have been run over by it as if by a truck, but his father whirled him around, pointed out the window and said, "There! Look! Look!"

Edward looked out the observatory windows, across the driveway. Back in the woods, down a little slope, a huge pine tree suddenly snapped in half and fell.

"Good shooting, Son! Good shooting!" His father clapped him on the back again, hard enough to send him staggering. Already he was choking from the smoke and gunpowder. His eyes stung. He tried to grope back to the spiral staircase. Then Father took him by the hand and led him away, through a door he hadn't noticed before, and suddenly they were standing in a very ordinary hallway.

He realized he was covered with gunpowder and soot.

"I—"

"That's right son. Go clean yourself up and change. Your mother doesn't like grubby boys at dinner."

Edward discovered another stairway and went down a single flight, and found himself somehow just outside the bathroom down the hall from his bedroom. As he cleaned himself he rehearsed his main theories—*I'm crazy, Dad's crazy, we're all crazy, this is a dream and I will wake up*—and came to no conclusion other than that he didn't think he was going to wake up any time soon. Whatever was going on, he was in for the duration.

He stared into the mirror. He wiped the gunpowder off his face with a washcloth.

It was only as he went down to dinner that it occurred to him to wonder whatever had happened to *lunch*. Well, nothing else made sense. Possibly time got lost in this crazy house like everything else.

He was the last one to sit down at the table. His father was there, looking scrubbed and neat and not wearing any captain's uniform.

"Busy day, Dear?" Mother said.

"Got things done. Found things out."

His father winked at Edward, who said nothing.

"I thought it was going to rain a while ago," Mother said.

"Oh?"

"Yes, I thought I heard thunder."

Chapter Three
A Desperately Normal Family Picnic

"I think we should have a *picnic!*" Edward's father boomed over the breakfast table.

"Today?" said Mom. "Don't we still have a lot of unpacking to do? Don't you have your work?"

"That'll keep! It can wait! Things will take care of themselves!" He startled to gesticulate, to wave his hands wildly. Edward knew that when he got that way, it was best to be ready to duck. "Why *not?* We're together, a normal family, on a lovely day, so it's a fine time for a picnic. Are there any dissenters? Anyone vote 'nay'?" He paused. "Unanimous. Motion carried! The entire family will report to the front driveway at eleven hundred hours *sharp!* Fun is obligatory! At ease! Carry on, troops! In the meantime, I *do* have some things to catch up on."

Father got up and left the room.

As Mom started to clear away the breakfast dishes, she simply said, "I guess we're going on a picnic today."

Edward shrugged. He glanced up at the ceiling, then out the window—it looked a bit overcast, perhaps not a fine day for a picnic, but it was going to have to do—and then said to Margaret, "Since when is this a normal family?"

She leaned over and whispered to him conspiratorially, "It's not good to be *too* normal, you know. Being too normal is *not normal*, so if you're *too normal* people will find out—that you're *not* normal. Got it?"

Edward broke up laughing so hard that he bent over double and nearly drowned himself in the remains of his cereal. There were moments like this when he actually thought his sister was funny, even clever, and he wasn't sure that younger brothers were supposed to regard older sisters like that. It wasn't normal. Which made it all that much funnier.

THE DRAGON HOUSE | 29

"I'm glad everyone is in such a good mood," Mom said.

"Yeah," said Edward, recovering somewhat. "Nice and normal."

Now Margaret was giggling.

As it worked out, the day was a passably good one for a picnic. A bit windy and chilly—it seemed to Edward that up here in the mountains it was *always* windy and chilly—but the clouds often broke to let the sunlight through and it didn't look like rain, at least not for several hours. Edward and Margaret both wore long jeans and sweatshirts and sneakers, as did Mom. It almost seemed a uniform. Edward decided that he would ask for a pair of mountaineering boots for his birthday (which was about two weeks away), but in the meantime, sneakers would have to do.

He carried a backpack, in which he had placed his binoculars, a couple jars for interesting specimens, should he come across any, and, more as a joke than anything else, his copy of *A Field Guide to American Monsters*.

Margaret helped carry their lunch, the smaller of two picnic baskets. Mom carried the other one.

"Are we READY?" It was Father who was not in uniform, or not in the same uniform. He came tramping down the front steps, out the front door, and into the driveway wearing a khaki shirt, khaki trousers that swelled out at the hips like old-time aviators used to wear, high, black boots, and an actual pith helmet the likes of which Edward had never seen outside of jungle movies. Father also had a backpack, containing Edward had no idea what, and carried a staff or hiking stick with an iron point on one end that he called an "alpenstock."

"Not *too* normal, are we?" Margaret whispered.

"I guess not."

Edward glanced over at the family SUV, parked in the driveway. His father poked him with the stick.

"Come, come, Edward! You don't think we're going to *drive* on our expedition, do you? No, this is a scouting mission, to learn the lay of the land. We *walk*."

"Okay, Dad. We walk," said Edward, not sure why his father put such emphasis on this.

"And remember everybody, *fun* will be had by all."

So they walked, and fun was had, though at first Edward had a creepy feeling as if someone or something were looking down on him as he walked away from the house. He turned back a couple times, and saw the house, huger than ever, with more complicated wings and towers and porticoes and gambles than he'd noticed before—he swore the place was *growing* and he'd never explore it all—and he had the distinct impression that something *was* watching him.

He noticed the square tower that he'd seen from his bedroom window. There were *four* gargoyles there now, one on each corner.

As soon as the house was out of sight and the family was alone in the woods, Edward felt more relaxed. No one said anything. They did *normal* things like tread very softly, trying to get close to a family of deer before the deer saw them and ran off.

The woods were deeper than any Edward had ever been in before. He'd only known city parks, and a stretch of the Pine Barrens when his family sometimes went over to New Jersey to swim in a lake and pick blueberries. These woods seemed to go on forever, and to drop away downhill on both sides, farther than he could see.

He realized that he was on one of those ridge-lines about which he'd had spooky thoughts on their drive up from Philadelphia. Civilization, *people,* were in the valleys. Here, up on the ridges, could be *anything,* and these ridges could go on forever.

But just now, with his family, with the sunlight streaming through the green leaves, it didn't seem a particularly scary notion that the woods went on forever. He imagined that he was a merman, gazing down into the depths of the sea. It would be so easy to let oneself drop down out of the shallows, over the edge of the continental shelf, and just descend. Maybe he'd never want to come back.

Later, through a break in the trees, they saw an eagle circling overhead.

Even Dad, who was normally so talkative, tended to be quiet in these woods. There was something about them that demanded silence. The trees closed overhead like the roof of a cathedral.

Then they came to a real clearing, the whole side of a hill which was almost without trees. There were dead ones, and broken stumps, but only scrub had grown up between them. In places, blueberries, like the ones Edward had seen in New Jersey, grew among rough grass.

He reached down to pick some berries, and a lizard scurried

away. It was indeed an interesting specimen, but he wasn't sure what he'd do with a live lizard just yet, and it was in any case too fast for him. He let it go.

Mom spread out a blanket and started to get out their lunch from the picnic baskets. Meanwhile, Edward and Margaret picked berries. He looked up as saw what must have been two more eagles, high overhead.

He stopped picking and just sat on a tree stump, gazing out over the landscape which stretched to the horizon, green and hilly and dotted with lakes, yet without any evidence that any human being had ever walked on the Earth. He was sure that there were highways down there, and towns, but from his present perspective he couldn't see them.

"Hey! Gone to sleep on us?"

Margaret nudged him. He resumed picking berries.

Later, as they sat and ate and stared out into the distance, Father promised a surprise. Edward was a little numb with surprises just new, after the experiences of the past couple days, and would have been content with just the woods and the view, but he knew there was going to be a surprise, and he had enough faith in his father to know it would be impressive.

After lunch, Dad started to undo his own backpack. He got out pieces of wood and metal, gleaming cloth with green scales on it, and more wire and clockwork and other stuff than reasonably could have fit into such a backpack. It was like one of those circus acts where the clown draws one handkerchief, and then another, and another, and a completely impossible number out of his sleeve.

Edward had previously asked his father if he was a magician.

Now he seemed to be a mechanic. Edward found himself pressed into service, screwing screws, tying strings, as they assembled something that looked like a light aircraft, but with gleaming scales all over it—a fish, no, it had wings—a dragon with a grinning face and long whiskers, like the ones that go parading through the streets on Chinese New Year.

Only this once was different. It was a surprise, as Father had promised.

This was no ordinary kite. There was more to it. Father lifted up the dragon's face as if it were a visor and revealed a brass pot with a lid on it. He opened the lid and poured in water from a canteen, then slid out the little attachment underneath which held a can of sterno. He lit the sterno with a cigarette lighter—the same one he'd used for the cannons, Edward realized; Father always seemed to carry it even though he didn't smoke.

Now the dragon was smoking, or steaming to be precise. Steam seeped out of its nostrils and mouth, like tentative puffs of breath. The contraption twitched of its own accord, fluttered its wings, and swished its tail from side to side, very much like a sleepy creature waking up.

Margaret and Mom stared with amazement. Edward was impressed, but was a little less amazed.

Father handed Edward a string and Margaret another. He took a third in hand himself, then said, "Come on! Let's get it flying!"

Almost before Edward realized what they were doing, all three of them were racing down the slope, leaping over rocks and fallen tree trunks, heaving the dragon into the air. It seemed to come more alive as they went, stretching its wings out to a good ten feet, its tail extending far longer. It caught the air. When Edward realized it was pulling against him, he let go, and his father and sister also let go, because this wasn't a kite. It was something that flew by itself, up, up, swirling around in circles, hissing and shooting sparks.

Dad yelled. Margaret got caught up in the excitement and yelled too. Edward watched silently as the dragon spiralled upward, swirling sparks. The two eagles overhead scattered in fright. Still the thing rose, but it didn't seem to diminish with distance, as if somehow it were getting *bigger* the higher it rose into the sky.

It let out a roar, and then, with a clap like thunder, vanished all of the sudden, leaving only a dissipating cloud of white smoke where it had been.

"Dad?" said Edward.

"Yes?"

"Was it supposed to do that?"

"Was it supposed to *blow up?*" Margaret suddenly interjected.

"What makes you think it did?" Dad said.

"Well, it, you know—"

"Went KA-BOOM," Edward said. "Now it's not there anymore."

Dad put his arms around both Edward and Margaret and said,

THE DRAGON HOUSE | 33

"Dragons are wise and powerful creatures. They are spiritual beings who take many forms. They are very close to immortal. When they disappear suddenly, it is because they've taken off faster than the eye can see. Sometimes they tear a hole in the sky. The result is more like a sonic boom. It is not an explosion. You don't see any *wreckage,* now, do either of you?"

Edward and Margaret both shook their heads.

"Dragons also can bring good luck to people who respect them, Edward. Look at this." Now Dad poked into the ground at Edward's feet with the toe of his boot. "Look what *you* found!"

Edward looked down to where his father's toe had knocked loose a greenish piece of stone, a flint. He recognized the shape at once. He dropped down and picked it up. *Yes!* It *was!* The finest Indian arrowhead he had ever seen!

He looked up at his father and could only mouth a silent "Wow," but then Dad was scooting Margaret back up the hill and both of them were running.

"Edward! It's time for dessert!" his father shouted.

When Edward caught up, Dad, Mom, and Margaret were already seated on the blanket again, eating slices of apple pie.

Edward showed off his arrowhead proudly.

"That's nice," Mom said.

He sat down and she handed him a paper plate with a piece of pie.

He didn't know what to say. It would have seemed silly to ask her if she'd seen the dragon, because of course she had.

"Your father has his ways," was all she said.

Their family was like that. Father could talk non-stop about anything and everything. He would get excited and jump up and down, and wave his arms. Mother remained calm. She said far less, but she had a way of summing up, of bringing things to a close with solid, good sense.

Father had his ways. He was given to creating dragons out of wood and scraps and setting them loose into the sky as if he were flying a kite.

For the Longstretch family, it didn't seem all that out of the ordinary, and there wasn't anything more to be said.

A bit later, Mom and Dad both suggested that Edward and Margaret might want to go exploring some more. There was enough of an implication that it was more than a suggestion, so that Edward and his sister quickly took the hint.

Sometimes their parents wanted to be alone to discuss something, and, indeed, as they started down a path into the woods, Edward could hear his father saying something about, "It's all happening too fast."

He didn't know what was happening too fast, but for the moment he tried not to worry about it. The woods closed around them again. They were still on the ridge-line, but it was narrower here, and soon they were climbing over a series of huge boulders placed in a row, almost as if they were part of a buried wall.

"I don't think we have to worry about being too normal," Margaret said after a while.

"Yeah."

"You do have to wonder, though."

"Uh-huh."

"Like, why are we here. What did they bring us to this crazy place? What kind of job does Dad have that means we all have to live here."

"Yeah."

Margaret stopped where she was. "Don't you know anything more than monosyllables?"

"I said 'Uh-huh.' That has two."

She reached out as if to smack him, but he ducked.

"You're as crazy as they are," she said. "Crazy as a bedbug."

"What *is* the sanity level of the average bedbug?" Edward said, balancing himself on a rock. "I mean, are they really more mentally disturbed than, say, the praying mantis or the dung beetle?"

"You know what I mean."

"Yeah."

Actually he knew far more. He and Dad had their secrets. He'd had very strange dreams so far. He hadn't told anyone. He wished he could confide in her, but she would just compare him to a bedbug again.

There were so many things he wanted to say but couldn't bring himself to say, to her, to his father, to his mother.

Instead he skipped from one rock to another, following what now looked like an old stone fence, until the ground leveled out and he found himself in a swampy clearing, ankle-deep in mud.

"How did *that* get here?" he said, more to himself than to her, because he was sure she didn't have any better idea than he did how, at the very end of the line of stones, at the tip of the tail of the mountain—he thought of it like that, the ridge-line tapering into a tail, which led him here—was a massive stone pillar on which squatted a stone gargoyle, a man-like figure with huge bat-wings, pointed ears, and a tail, very much like the ones he'd seen from his bedroom window.

It was all he could do not to say "Jeepers," which would have embarrassed him to no end in front of his sister.

Margaret reached out.

"Don't touch it!"

But she did. Lichen and moss crumbled away at her fingertips. It seemed to be just stone, but Edward himself was reluctant to touch it.

"I guess it was put here by the same crazy people who built our house," Margaret said.

"Maybe we ought to get back," Edward said.

They made their way back, along the stones, up the ridgeline, into the sloping clearing, where they found that their parents had packed everything up and were waiting for them.

"I think," said their father, "that this expedition has reached its conclusion, and we should return to base to correlate the data gathered."

"Yeah, Dad," Edward said, somewhat out of breath.

So they walked back to the house, saying little. After a while the sky finally did cloud over, and it began to rain, a light drizzle rattling through the leaves overhead. Only once in a while did Edward feel a drop on his face.

Despite everything, he realized, this had been a more or less normal day for himself and for his family, and he had a sinking feeling that he might not see anything nearly as normal again for some time to come.

Chapter Four
All At Once and Way Too Fast

The next morning Edward woke up and stuck his hand right through the wall of his bedroom. He had, after all, only slept in this room for a couple of nights, and so, half asleep, he forgot which side of the bed he was supposed to get out on, rolled the wrong way, and before he knew it his hand was *in* the wall.

The sensation was just like the steering wheel the other night, first a tingling, then his hand was sinking into matter as warm and sticky as molasses, and he was *part* of something far larger than himself. He heard wind whistling in his ears. Particularly when he closed his eyes he seemed to see in all directions at once, the wooded landscape, the lake in the distance, and also the interior of the house itself: a jumble of rooms he had never seen before, and, below, a series of cellars that went far down into the earth, much farther than cellars really should.

It felt as if he were flying and falling at the same time.

Something down in the cellar stirred and opened its eyes and stared back at him.

He shook his head. By opening his eyes, and concentrating very hard, he could see only the bedroom, his museum and books, the Fokker Triplane, the sunlight streaming through odd, porthole-shaped window; but he still was sitting up in bed, with his left hand *in* the wall.

"Whoa..." he said aloud, and he drew his hand out of the wall.

The extra sensations ceased, and he was just Edward, sitting in bed, in a sunlit bedroom, staring down at his own hand. The only sounds were of the house creaking slightly, and of crows cawing outside.

He wriggled his fingers. He didn't seem hurt, any more than he had been after the experience with the wheel.

So he stuck his hand back in the wall.

He found that he had to do it deliberately. He had to press, and *think* beyond the wall, and then his hand would sink in, and he felt, again, part of a larger body or being, as if he had extra eyes and extra ears and were in several places at the same time.

The thing in the cellar was still there, looking up at him. Its eyes glowed red in the dark, but somehow he wasn't afraid of it. He was uncertain, as he had been when he had first stood in the driveway looking up at the house. It was, again, like meeting a large, strange dog on a forest path.

Both of them looked at the other, waiting for the other to make a move.

He was sure this wasn't a dog.

"Edward..." it said, its voice inside his ears like muted thunder.

"You know my name?"

"Edward," it said again, and then closed its eyes and seemed to go back to sleep.

"Huh?"

He pulled his hand out of the wall.

He swivelled around and placed a bare foot on the floor. He wondered what would happen if—

No, he wasn't ready for that yet. He drew his foot back up and sat in bed, contemplating the wall.

He stuck his hand back in the wall. Though distracted by the flood of new sensations, he noticed that he could only push it in as far as the sleeve of his pajama top. So, with his free hand, he rolled the sleeve up, and pushed his arm in all the way up to the elbow.

Now everything he felt was much more intense. He was seeing, hearing, and feeling in other places.

He thought of the neat tricks he could do with this. He could hide stuff in the wall. He could do "magic" and produce a rabbit, not out of a hat, but out of the wall.

He pulled his arm out again, but only long enough to roll up his right sleeve. Then he pressed *both* hands into the wall, and suddenly he felt as if his arms were a mile long, as if he could reach and touch things far away in the house. He turned a doorknob somewhere in the attic and opened a closet. He heard, but did not quite see, a pile of boxes fall out. With his other hand he reached *somewhere else* and ran his fingers over a series of heavy, cold glass jars.

What he did next was, he knew, crazy, definitely against his "better judgement"—a phrase he had heard his parents using, but he was not entirely sure that boys his age had better judgement.

He pressed his face against the wall. At first this just squashed his nose, but then he went *through,* his entire head, until he was caught by his shoulders, right at the collar of his pajama top.

For half a second he was afraid he wouldn't be able to breathe, but that wasn't a problem. Indeed, it was like flying. If he closed his own eyes, and let some *other* eyes see for him, he seemed to be soaring over the hills and trees, above the clouds, and diving into the earth, layers of stone rushing past him.

But if he opened his eyes, deliberately, the way you learn to do underwater, he was looking *inside* the house, at a dark mass of wood and stone, twisting stairways and empty rooms, all of which seemed to ripple and sway and drift. It was very much like looking into water.

If he concentrated a little, he could direct his vision, and see into specific rooms. His head seemed to pop up out of the floor into that deserted bedroom above his own—the old lady's room, he called it—and he saw everything he'd seen there before, but from the perspective of being down on the floor. Then he pulled back, and let himself sink, and he saw his mother below in the kitchen making breakfast.

He saw a room he'd never seen before, tall, with long sunlit windows like the inside of a church, but filled with every conceivable sort of clock, all of them ticking and whirring away.

And he saw his sister, sitting up in her bed, legs crossed, typing away on her laptop.

He called out to her, "Hey Mags! Look at me!"

She stopped, and looked around, as if she wasn't sure she'd heard something.

"Hey Mags!"

She looked again, hesitating, then went back to her typing.

He found that if he pushed very hard he could reach out and touch one of the books on her shelf.

He knocked it onto the floor.

Now, clearly startled, Margaret stopped typing and looked up again. She was listening.

"Mags!"

"Edward?"

She put her computer down and got off the bed. She went to the door of her room, opened it, and leaned out into the hall.

"Edward? Did you call?"

"Yes, I did," he said, "but not from over there!"

But she didn't hear that, and, still puzzled, went to pick up the fallen book.

While her back was turned he reached out of the wall and typed on her computer. He saw that his hands and arms, extending from the wall, were not skin-colored at all, but more like living wood. It was very strange indeed.

Nevertheless he typed, in the middle of whatever document she had been working on, "HI MAGS, IT'S EDWARD. NYUCK, NYUCK, NYUCK."

The last part was a special tease, since he liked the Three Stooges after his father had so enthusiastically introduced them to the family on DVD. Neither Margaret nor their mother had been much taken by the Stooges. Mom explained that it was a boy thing, for big boys or small ones, and Margaret had said, "Yeah, a birth-defect linked to the y-chromosome."

After one last "NYUCK" Edward drew his hands back into the wall, just in time for his sister to stare wide-eyed at the screen and say aloud, "Edward! How did you do that?"

The thing was, she knew he didn't *have* a computer. He was supposed to get one for his next birthday, in time for the 9th grade. So he couldn't have hacked in somehow. He left her to figure that one out.

He pulled his arms and his face out of the wall. Then he heard someone calling his name.

"Edward! Edward! Time for breakfast!"

It was just Mom at the base of the stairs.

He got out of bed and stood on the floor. The floorboards seemed to yield just a bit, as if he were walking on a trampoline—no, the floor felt almost alive, like the hide of an enormous animal. An image flashed into his head, of one of those tiny birds that lives on the back of a hippotamus.

But he didn't sink in. He walked unsteadily over to the bedroom door.

"Edward!"

"Coming, Mom!" he yelled back.

He went downstairs as he was, in his pajamas with the sleeves rolled up, and barefoot. The floor and the railing and the wall he ran his hand along felt like wood, but somehow, indefinably, a little different.

When he got to the kitchen, everyone was already seated around the little breakfast table.

Margaret stared at him. He wasn't sure if she was angry or afraid or just what.

"Well, aren't we the sleepy one!" Mom said, grabbing hold of him and mussing his already quite messy hair.

Everybody else was already dressed.

Edward sat down without a word and dug in to his eggs and pancakes.

"I am sure you will have an energetic day," Mom said. "Wide awake. Lots to do."

"Yeah," he said.

Then Dad started to babble on as he sometimes did, talking more to himself than to the family, about angles and spheres and how the outer conjunctions were coming together a lot sooner than expected, and Edward had absolutely no idea what he was talking about. Margaret said nothing and watched Edward as if he were some strange animal about to do something unexpected. Eventually Mom said to Dad, "I don't think we need to talk about that over breakfast."

"No," he said after a pause. "I guess not."

Dad picked the newspaper, took out the sports section, made a big show of rustling it, raising the paper up until it hid him from the rest of the family, and then he folded it back down, looked over the top straight at Edward, and said, "Hey, how about those Phillies?"

"Dad, I don't like baseball."

"Well, Son, you don't want people to think you are *odd*."

"What people, Dad?"

"Well…" he gestured uncertainly around the room, as if trying to indicate people who weren't there. "The neighbors. The people in town."

"But we're not in Philadelphia anymore," said Edward. "Shouldn't we be rooting for a team called the Badgers or the Squirrels or something?"

"Or the Cows?" said his sister.

"You may have a point," Dad said.

THE DRAGON HOUSE | 41

Margaret said nothing for the rest of breakfast. She just sat there, eyeballing Edward as if he were very odd indeed.

* * * *

When he got back to his room, Edward did something that was admittedly odd, even to himself. He stood still in the middle of the floor. Since they had just moved in and had hardly unpacked, there was no rug, so he let his feet sink into the bare boards. He sank to his ankles, right to the cuffs of his pajama bottoms. When he walked, the floorboards rippled, like scum on the surface of a pond, but the sensation was more than that. He was outside himself again. It was as if he could feel the very foundations of the house gripping the earth and stones below, and he could feel the roots of every tree.

His head was spinning with thoughts that were not quite his own, or at least he didn't know where they were coming from. An idea formed, a kind of plan, something that sorted itself out of the confusion. He knew what he was supposed to do.

He leaned on his dresser. *That* was solid enough. His hand did not sink into it, *because it was not part of the house,* he somehow understood.

He leaned down and opened the bottom drawer and got out an old pair of swimming trunks that he'd almost outgrown. They were so brief on him that he was usually embarrassed to wear them, but they were exactly what he needed now.

He sat down on his bed, took off his pajamas, and put on the trunks, and nothing else. He pulled the drawstrings tight and tied them.

He sat down on the edge of the bed and drew his feet up, then waited for the rushing sounds in his ears to stop. He tried to think clearly, but there was nothing left to think about. He knew that he was already on his course, like a pinball rolling down the chute.

Just as he'd been taught to do in swimming lessons, he crouched on the edge of the bed, swaying a little, with his arms stretched out in front of him, hands folded, head down, ears covered by his arms, and he just leaned forward and plunged *into* the floor. Not onto it, *into* it.

At first he felt a tug at his waist and a stinging blow to his stomach as if he'd just done a bellyflop into a pool, but then something seemed to give way, to pop, and he was through and moving freely. He reached back once to reassure himself that he hadn't lost his trunks. They were fine.

He was floating in darkness. He breathed in great gasps. He could smell, very intensely, the smells of the earth and of leaves and of the woods, and the dust of dry attics and empty rooms, and the dampness of the deep cellars. Cold wind blew against his bare skin and buffeted him about like a bird that didn't quite know how to fly. He was both high up in the sky and below the ground at the same time.

Just like the house, from highest rooftop to the lowest foundation.

He waved his arms and kicked and managed to stabilize himself. It was a bit like swimming, only through something thicker than water. His body seemed to have become rubbery, like something in a cartoon, so that he could ooze through tight spots or ripple down a flight of stairs like spilled water.

He could see again, but differently, almost as if he were wearing infra-red goggles, all browns and reds and blacks, with a great deal of shadow, as if objects slowly rose out of the darkness to reveal themselves to his view. Nevertheless he knew everything around him. He could feel walls and doorknobs and the backs of chairs, old lamps, books on shelves, as if he were touching them all simultaneously.

He swam down until his face and arms and shoulders emerged from the ceiling of a closet. He groped in darkness, finding hangers, coats, boxes on the shelves. He drew back into the ceiling and let himself drift horizontally for a while, as if he were carried by a current. He looked down and saw his mother seated at the kitchen table, reading the newspaper after she'd finished with the breakfast dishes.

He didn't call out to her. She wasn't ready for this, he decided. It probably hadn't been a good idea to play the prank on Margaret, and he was sure his mother's reaction would be a lot worse.

Nevertheless he reached down and grabbed an old-fashioned metal salt-shaker off a top shelf and tried to draw it up into the ceiling. It wouldn't come. He pulled, and the salt-shaker tapped gently against the plaster.

Mom looked up at the sound but didn't seem to realize where it was coming from.

He tugged again, gently. No good. This was interesting to know. *He* could merge into the walls, but he couldn't bring foreign objects in with him. He'd only managed with the swimming trunks because he was wearing them and he had dragged them in from the sheer force of his dive. Maybe if he clutched something to his chest and *ran* into a wall, he would likewise be able to move small items from room to room, but the salt-shaker, too large for him to make a fist around, just held in the tips of his fingers, wasn't going anywhere.

He tried to put it back on the shelf, but missed. The salt-shaker fell to the floor with a clatter.

Quickly Edward drew his hand back up into the ceiling and lay there, absolutely still, hoping he wouldn't be noticed. Fortunately Mother looked down at the salt-shaker, not up at the ceiling.

There was still a "current" around him, almost like a pulse. He surrendered to it and let it carry him away.

Now he was sinking into darkness, passing through many rooms and hallways he had never seen before, but which he felt as if they were a part of him. He felt the cool, wet stone as he sank deep into the foundations of the house.

Something throbbed in front of him, down below, like the beating of an enormous heart.

Then the bright, burning eyes he had seen before opened before him, and the same voice whispered inside his head, *"Edward, you are welcome. We meet at last."*

He was more afraid than not just now. He came to rest on a damp stone floor, in a cold, dark place. He wasn't merged with the walls or the stones anymore. He was out in the air, standing in an underground chamber of some sort on rough, hard stones that hurt his feet, shivering, wearing just a pair of swimming trunks while the two enormous, red eyes floated before him, and something huge seemed to move and shift in the darkness.

A suit of armor and a sword might have been appropriate right now, but he didn't have any.

He hugged his shoulders and shook his knees. It was hard to imagine how he could have been made to feel any more vulnerable.

Then an enormous mouth opened beneath the eyes, like a Cheshire cat grin, only somehow almost human, even if the teeth were longer than he was tall, sharp, and glowing bright orange.

That was how.

The mouth began to speak.

"Edward Eusebius Longstretch, my brave Edward. We shall be

companions on journeys into the darkness. We shall travel to strange worlds and fight battles in vast wars among the stars, you and I, who are as one, who have such an...affinity."

"We shall?" said Edward in a tiny voice, just above a whisper. "We do?"

"Let me have a closer look at you, my newly-arrived Edward."

The floor shook beneath his feet and a section in front of him—about the size of a small football field, it looked to him—started to rise, and gradually shaped itself into an enormous outstretched *claw*.

The forefinger or foreclaw curled, beckoning him.

There was no help for it. He couldn't escape. Possibly he was brave Edward after all.

He stepped up onto the beckoning finger, and the thing raised him up, even as he might raise a tiny bug on the tip of his finger.

If the monster wanted to eat him, there wasn't much he could do about it.

Instead, it breathed on him gently. Its breath was sulfurous and warm, but the smell of it left his throat sore and his eyes running. It was all he could do not to gag and cough.

And he saw the enormous face then, clearly, spiked, stony ridges above the eyes, an extended, rough snout sort of like a crocodile's, but with an upper lip that curved down like a beak that looked like it could bite the Empire State Building in half.

It was a dragon's face. He did not doubt that this was a real, live dragon. After all he had seen in the past couple of days, he could only think, *Why not?*

"Hello, Edward."

"Uh, hello?"

"Do you know who I am, Edward?"

"Do I?"

The thing breathed on him again, and the wind of its breath knocked him off his feet. For an instant he was afraid he would fall, but he landed safely, sitting down, his back against the dragon's claw, what would have been a long fingernail on a human. It felt like steel, only warm. The skin beneath him was halfway between leathery and a mass of rough stones.

Suddenly, somehow, he *did* know. His senses were, again, more than his own, as they were when he first put his hand into the wall or even the first time he'd taken hold of the steering wheel at his father's direction on the balcony outside the library.

He could see farther into the darkness than his eyes otherwise could have. He had more than one perspective. He was both a dragon gazing at a tiny mite of a boy sitting on his fingertip, and that boy looking into the darkness, perceiving the dragon—both with sight and more than sight. He saw the enormous ridges of its neck muscles extending into the gloom and distance, merging with the stone of the cavern, with the earth itself, and he understood that this dragon was like an enormous *turtle,* which wore the house and the hilltop the house stood on and the whole ridgeline he and his sister had followed to its very tip the other day on their picnic *like a shell.*

The house and the ridge and the dragon were *all one,* alive, one body, and he, Edward, had a strange affinity, which allowed him to feel as it did, as if he were lying buried in the ground, his body stretched out for miles and weighing unimaginable tons, and he could feel the trees growing out of him, slowly, their roots seeking down into his flesh, but part of him, too. At the same time he felt the wind passing over the trees and he heard the cries of the eagles circling hard overhead.

"Pleased to meet you, Edward," said the *Dragon House.* It moved its fingertip around slowly before its enormous, burning eyes. *"Our lives and our destinies are one, and we have much to talk about, but—wait, you have to go now. Your father is calling."*

Without another word, before Edward could say more than "But—" it flung him upward, the way you would release a flying beetle, and again he was swimming through stone and wood and through the very walls of the house. He caught a brief glimpse of a cellar the size of an aircraft hangar, but with vaulting, stone arches and filled with strange, rusty machinery. He rose through many other rooms. He saw his mother alone in her room with a Fred Astaire tape on the VCR, practicing dance steps.

He rose up.

"Edward—"

It was his father calling.

"Dad! I'm coming!" he called back.

Chapter Five
Explanations That Explain Nothing

Edward broke through the floor like a swimmer coming up from a long dive. He gasped for breath instinctively, although he'd been able to breathe fine all the way.

His father caught him under the shoulders and lifted him to his feet, as if out of a pool of something thick and sticky. Edward watched with uneasy fascination as the dark brown, wooden color drained away down his chest and stomach, then from his legs and feet, until he was no longer *part* of the house but merely in it, standing barefoot on a rough and splintery floor, very underdressed in front of a group of strangers, in a room he'd never seen before.

His father wore his captain's outfit, which looked rather like a band costume.

Another man, tall, and gray-haired, with a short, silvery beard, and a hard look to his eyes, leaned forward. He was dressed entirely in black, complete with black gloves and a black top hat in his hand. The only trace of color on him was a golden watch-chain, which looped from his lapel to a breast pocket. He seemed to be studying Edward as one might a newly discovered species of bird or insect.

Edward felt embarrassed in such formal company, and unthinkingly tried to cover himself with his hands.

"Get the boy something to wear," the man said to Dad, and Dad rummaged about in a closet until he came back with a rough and plain brown robe that tied shut across the chest with leather cords, exactly the sort of thing a wizard's apprentice might wear. Edward slid the robe over his head, but it was way too large, and fell in a pile at his feet, so if he wanted to walk he to fold some of it over his left arm the way an ancient Roman would when wearing a toga.

"I see, young man," said the man in black, in a strange accent that seemed to thicken with every word he spoke, for all that his speech was never other than precise and perfectly articulated, "that you have figured out the first principle of your situation, or condition, or perhaps I should call it a relationship with the house. I refuse to call it a predicament. Nevertheless, you have clearly gotten to square one, and are to be congratulated."

"I have? I am?"

The stranger leaned down and whispered to Edward with great intensity, as if revealing a deep secret, *"Flesh must touch for magic to be true."*

His nearness was so alarming that Edward stepped backwards, tripped over his robe, and fell down with a thud.

He sat up, but did not immediately get up. He realized he was in the middle of a chalk circle with strange signs written all around it, as if he'd been conjured there.

He sat cross-legged, wrapping the robe around himself defensively.

"Wha...tt...my colleague...mea...ns...to say..." Another person spoke suddenly, and Edward turned to face a figure far more alarming than the first, a hunched, trembling shape in a green robe with a hood that entirely hid the wearer's face. This person moved with a clicking, whirring, scraping sound, very much, Edward thought, like a broken robot staggering toward the repair shop.

But when this person hit himself on the side of the head, as if to make an adjustment, the hood fell back revealing a face that seemed more insect-like than human, triangular, with huge eyes, wriggling antennae, and a mouth that twitched and drooled like that of a grasshopper or praying mantis.

Even so, Edward wasn't even sure it was alive. It looked mechanical. The drool might well be oil.

The bump on the head seemed to have cleared up its (or just possibly his) speech, which was now rapid, fluent, almost cheerful.

"What my colleague means, is that you must *touch* the magical thing to be in communion with it—*in touch* with it, you might say. In your case, the house. When you touch, the *more* you touch, as you have indeed figured out, the more you and the house—*and the dragon* are all *one and the same.* Understand?"

"No, not really..."

Dad spoke up. "You must pardon us, Edward. Introductions are in order."

The man in black held out his hand. Edward got to his feet uncertainly and took it.

"I am Doctor Basileus, at your service, Edward. Captain of the first rank, Watchers Guild."

Edward didn't know what to say or ask.

"We watch dragons," the man said.

"And I," said the insect-faced thing, "am Zarcon of the planet Zarconax."

It did not hold out its hands. It wriggled its fingers instead. Perhaps that was a form of greeting. Edward noticed that Zarcon of Zarconax wore gloves. He wasn't sure how many fingers there were.

Somehow after all that had happened in the past couple of days, meeting a being from outer space didn't faze Edward. He wasn't sure he'd ever be surprised again.

"And you—you watch dragons too?"

"No, Edward. I watch people who *touch* dragons, who can communicate with them and perhaps even control them. People like yourself, people for whom the dragons have an *affinity*. You do not yet realize how extraordinary you are."

"I guess not."

"Not everyone can put his hand through a wall, Edward, not even in this house. I can't." Zarcon of Zarconax shambled over to the nearest wall, rapped on it, and came back. "I can much less...*swim* inside them, as you were doing."

"What my learned associate is attempting to explain, Edward," said Doctor Basileus, "is that when you have touched a thing and become *part* of it, that is the *first step*. To wholly immerse yourself is something you may wish to continue under circumstances, something you might even enjoy, but when you become more practiced, you can achieve the same effect with the touch of a single hand, or even wearing gloves. Only the most accomplished masters can do it with gloves on."

Edward noticed again that all of them, including his father, were wearing gloves.

"That may be because they don't have hands anymore," said Zarcon of Zarconax suddenly. Then his (or its—Edward was not sure precisely *what* Zarcon was) voice suddenly lapsed into a squeal and a scratching sound, like a broken phonograph. One more slap to the side of the head fixed that. Zarcon *smiled* if that were possible and said, "What I mean is, don't try any fire spells yet, kid, until you know what you're doing."

"I won't."

Dad put his hand on Edward's shoulder and said, "Come here, Son." Edward gathered up enough of his robe to walk and let himself be led off the wooden floor in the middle of the room to a cold stone floor at the edge. There was a large window with a broad sill. If a castle could be said to have a bay window, this was it.

Edward sat down and leaned over to look out. He was higher up than he had ever been in the house, in one of the towers. It seemed to be late afternoon, the sky overcast. He could still see for miles. About a hundred feet below, against a balcony, an airship of some kind lay tethered, sort of like a blimp but with odd wings and strangely ornate propellers on both the front and back. Presumably Dr. Basileus and Zarcon had arrived in this.

His father and Dr. Basileus stood before him, towering over him, all except Zarcon, who was only about four feet tall.

"It wasn't supposed to be this way Edward," Dad said. "I'm *sorry*. Things were supposed to happen a lot more gradually, over a series of years, not days. Much of what you now must learn, we weren't supposed to tell you until you had grown up."

Now Edward was beginning to get genuinely scared. He had never heard his father speak to him in quite that tone before. Certainly he had never heard him *apologize* like that before. He pulled his feet up into the windowsill and huddled inside the brown robe. He felt a sudden chill that wasn't entirely from the cold.

"Edward, we are in the middle of a war," said Dr. Basileus. "It is taking place now, on the Earth, in the sky, throughout the universe between forces you might imprecisely but conveniently refer to as Light and Darkness. We are—*you* are—on the side of Light, I hasten to reassure you. But whom, or exactly what, we serve remains an unknowable mystery. There many layers of being above us, many creatures greater and wiser than any of us, and more above them, and more above them, very likely unto infinity."

"Like a mountain in mist," said Zarcon of Zarconax. "The bottom is very impressive, even if you cannot see the top."

"Nor can you see the bottom of the pit from which our enemies rise. As above, so below," said Dr. Basileus, his voice assuming an even more somber tone than before.

None of this made a great deal of sense to Edward. "Does this mean we're working for…God? And the other side is the Devil?"

"We simply don't know, Edward," Dad said slowly.

"But what has this got to do with *me?*"

"Absolutely everything," said Dr. Basileus. "Absolutely everything has to do with, and centers on, *you.*"

"Edward," said Zarcon of Zarconax, in a rapid, clipped manner that had a rat-tat-tat sound to it. "The problem is. The matter is. The Dragon House is *awake.* Right now. It was supposed to go on sleeping, dreaming, for *years* yet. But we have been discovered. *Found.*"

This still made very little sense to Edward.

"Found? Who found us?"

"Edward, come here," said Dr. Basileus.

Edward got up from the windowsill. He heaved a large fold of the robe he was wearing over his arm and shuffled forward.

Suddenly Zarcon started chittering and shaking. "But first! But first! The danger!"

Edward stood still. *What danger?* He mouthed the words but did not speak aloud. None of this seemed quite real to him. It was all too strange.

"Ah," said Dr. Basileus. "You are correct to remind me. Now is as good a time as any. Edward, I have something for you." He took out a thin golden case from an inside pocket of his jacket and opened it, drawing out what looked like a medal on a thin chain. Without any ceremony or words he lowered the chain over Edward's head.

Edward took the medal or whatever it was in his hand and tried to examine it, then let go suddenly with a startled "Hey!" when he felt the chain around his neck *shrinking.* He tried to tear it off, but Dr. Basileus caught hold of his hand and stopped him.

"It's all right. It's not going to choke you. It is merely adjusting itself."

Edward explored with his free hand and found that the chain was still loose enough around his neck that he could slide a finger under it, but the medallion or whatever it was rested right at the base of his throat, at the top of his collar-bone. If he leaned his head down, he could almost touch it with his chin, but he couldn't see it. The thing was slightly rough and warm to the touch. It felt a little like metal, but not quite. He looked up at Dr. Basileus questioningly.

"It is a golden scale of the King Dragon, Edward. It will protect you. You must never take it off. It may become useful sooner than you expect."

"I don't think I'll be able to."

It might have seemed sensible to ask "What King Dragon?" but Edward was beginning to feel a bit overwhelmed.

"Indeed, yes, you want to know," said Zarcon of Zarconax. "You want to know—you are laughing at this—"

Edward did not realize anything of the sort, but suddenly the thought *did* seem funny.

"—whether or not the world I come from is named after me or I after my world. I must be very important to have a name like that. Yes, yes, important, but not like that. *Everyone* on Zarconax is named Zarcon, which would be confusing except that each of us pronounces his name *slightly differently*, which is fine for us, confusing for you, just as well that I am the only representative of my species present. You want to know about the King Dragon, too. Yes. It is the greatest of all dragons, the father of all dragons, the dragon that lies in the center of the universe, within the light that blinds us to gaze upon. We, you, I, my colleagues, are all servants of the King Dragon, even as the King Dragon serves That Which Is Beyond, which none of us may know or name. Yes. Yes. You are thinking as you stand there wiggling your toes on the wooden floor that this is all crazy and maybe you should just sink down through the floor again and go back to playing games in the walls, but no, no, it's not as easy as that. You're quite right that swimming around like that is going to be inconvenient when winter comes. I can only suggest that you place appropriate clothing in every closet in the house so you won't catch a nasty cold…you are wondering if I can read your mind—"

"Uh, yes," said Edward.

"I can. When you are close by. Particularly if we *touch.*"

Zarcon reached out and caught Edward by the wrist, which startled him. Edward broke away.

"Enough of that," said Dr. Basileus. "The boy must learn these things slowly."

"There is no time for slowly!" said Zarcon of Zarconax.

"More immediately to the point, Edward," Dad said. "Come over here. Look at this."

Edward followed him across the room, to a space behind a series of large book-cases, where Dad drew back a curtain from a large, oval window.

"Look, Edward. This may seem like just a made-up story to you, or maybe you think we've all gone insane, but I am afraid the problem is more immediate than that."

Edward looked. From this perspective, he knew where he was. He gazed across a sweep of rooftops and gables, down on what he thought of as the observatory, the room he had been in with his father before, the one with the bulging glass domes for windows that reminded him of enormous insect-eyes. The room with the balcony, the steering wheel, and the cannons.

Only now something dark and terrible swarmed over the glass, a great number of somethings, a mass of wriggling shapes that somehow looked halfway between human figures in flowing black robes and gigantic leeches. Their numbers increased even as he watched. They seemed to materialize out of the air, as if leaking into this world from somewhere else. He felt a shudder of horror just to look on them at this distance, as if he knew, more instinctively than through reason, that these things were *bad news,* the very essence of everything he could possibly fear.

"We've been discovered, Edward. We were not ready for this."

Suddenly one of the things detached itself from the mass and hurled through the air directly at them.

Before Edward could shout more than "Look out!" it smacked hard against the oval glass, which fortunately did not crack. Edward and the others all lurched back, then looked in uneasy fascination as the thing was revealed in detail, pressed against the window like a specimen on a slide.

It was a little bit like a man, Edward decided. At least it had discernable arms and legs—with enormous, overlong, deathly pale hands, fingers three or four times as long as human fingers and ending in sharp claws—but he could not quite tell if it was wearing loose, flowing clothing, or if the black filmy stuff swirling around it was part of its body, like the mass of a jellyfish.

The face was the worst part. The mouth was like a lamprey's, like a huge suction-cup with teeth all the way around it. This spread out impossibly far, pulsating, sucking and scratching at the window glass, while behind it two pale, burning eyes radiated sheer hatred.

Edward had to turn away. "What *is* it?"

"The common term," said Dr. Basileus, "is Ghastly Horror. It is certainly descriptive enough. That—those, all of them, are Ghastly Horrors. You will find a volume in the library your father showed you, entitled *Ghastly Horrors and What To Do About Them.* I recommend that you study it at your earliest possible convenience. These are but the least of the enemies we must now confront. They are just minions, servants, messengers."

"They can bite your head off, too," said Zarcon of Zarconax.

Edward stood uneasily, fingering the dragon scale around his neck.

As he did, there came another thumping sound. Another Ghastly Horror had now attached itself to the other window they'd been looking out earlier.

"We're surrounded," said Edward. "What are we going to do?"

"I don't doubt they're all over the house by now," Dad said. That didn't sound reassuring at all.

"What we must do," said Dr. Basileus, "is marshall our forces. Study. Learn. Gather what powers we have to ourselves in our defense."

"Which means what?" Edward asked.

"We'll be all right," Dad said quickly, "as long as we stay inside and they're outside. Don't go out and we'll be okay—"

A horrible thought came to Edward. "What about Mom and Margaret?"

"They'll be okay too, if they stay indoors."

"Did anybody warn them?" Edward screamed.

"Uh, well, I—I—"

"Mom! Mags!" Edward broke away from his father, dodged around Dr. Basileus and Zarcon of Zarconax, and ran, his long robe bunched up under his arm. He circled the room, looking for a way out. He yanked open one door. It was a closet. Several glowing crystal skulls like the one he had seen in the library the other night tumbled off a top shelf, grumbling, "Hey! Hey! Watch it!"

He yanked open another door, revealing a stairway, and hurried down it so quickly that inevitably some of the robe slipped out of his grasp, and he tripped over it, and fell tumbling down the stairs, somersaulting head over heels, banging head, elbows, and knees against the steps and the walls, until he came to rest at the bottom.

Even then he didn't hesitate for an instant, but hauled himself up, gathered the apprentice's robe into a bundle in both of his hands, and ran down a hallway, through several rooms without noting much of their contents (although one seemed to be full of stuffed birds that stirred their wings and twittered as he went by), until he found another stairway. He made his way down this one without falling again, all the while shouting "Mom! Mom! Mags! Look out!"

There were more rooms. Off to one side, through a wide-open door, he saw the carousel room. He almost knew where he was.

"Mom!"

He made his way down yet another stairway, his bare feet pounding on the stairs. He fell again and rolled, then sat up and realized that he was outside his own bedroom.

"Mom!"

But there was no answer.

He heard a sound from inside his room.

"Mags?"

Something stirred. Something fell, probably a book from a shelf.

He opened the door and looked in.

For a moment he didn't know what he was looking at. It was as if the floor of his room were somehow covered with a thick mass of bubbling, black tar, but then as he watched the blackness *stood up* to form something that was vaguely manlike but so tall that it hunched down beneath the ceiling.

"Hello Edward," it said with its lamprey-mouth, like a trumpet of flesh lined with teeth. "It seems your sister wanted to get better reception for her wireless internet, so she opened the window of her room—"

Edward yelled and tried to run, but he tripped over the robe again as enormous white fingers like foot-long, wriggling snakes caught hold of him, and sharp claws dug into him. He kicked and twisted, but the grip only tightened and the pain from the claws only got worse.

The thing spread itself out, the formless mass of its body extending into enormous bat-like wings, and with a leap it hurled through the port-hole window in Edward's room, smashing out the glass and a good deal of the wall besides, carrying him off into space.

Chapter Six
Winged Horrors and an Orange Jumpsuit

Edward's captor bore him high into dark clouds, into the cold upper air. Lightning flashed around him. Soon they were driving through howling wind and frigid rain.

Possibly the monster had sprouted more than one pair of hands. It held him firmly under his arms, its claws pressing into his chest and shoulders, alternately squeezing him and relaxing slightly between each stroke of its great wings until he could barely breathe. He twisted and tried to struggle, but the thing also seemed to have him just as firmly around the waist. He could only hang limply in its clutches. As he looked down, he saw only his useless robe trailing behind him like a flag, and below that, darkness.

His teeth chattered and he wept, from cold and pain and mostly from the dreadful fear that he had failed to warn his mother and sister, and that something terrible had happened to them, *because of him.*

It wasn't as if something terrible were not happening to him *right now* because his father and his father's colleagues had failed to warn *him.* That was too much to think about right now. Nothing made sense.

He tried to ask his captor where they were going. He shouted. Either it could not hear him or it just didn't want to answer.

He didn't imagine they were headed anywhere he'd ever want to be.

He lost all sense of time. He didn't know how long they had been flying or how far. Perhaps he passed out for a while.

Once a bolt of lightning split the sky and they seemed to ride down it, like a surfer down a wave, sparks flying like spray, the glare so intense that Edward had to shut his eyes, the heat burning him.

Then darkness closed around them again like a door slamming shut. They hurtled on through the wind and the rain. The Ghastly Horror swayed from side to side, sometimes almost rolling over, swinging Edward in wide, dizzying arcs.

A particularly strong blast buffeted them and the monster momentarily *lost its grip.* Edward felt himself falling. The thing caught him again, awkwardly, by one leg, around his middle. His robe started to tear. Edward slipped again, within it.

He got one hand free and frantically clung to his captor.

Just then one of its claws raked across his chest and touched the golden chain and the dragon scale around his neck.

The Ghastly Horror let out a *shriek* as if it had been burned and tried to *shake him off,* which was the worst yet, because Edward knew he must be thousands of feet up in the air. His robe was tearing to shreds. He slipped more. The creature rolled and wriggled, suddenly trying to be rid of him. The best he could do was cling to his captor. He had a firm grip around what must have been an ankle and held on with all his strength. He wasn't sure how many legs it had now, two, maybe three. Something heavy hit him across the back. That might have been a tail. But it did not dislodge him.

Down both of them fell, the monster swirling around and around like a falling leaf, unable to maintain its flight with Edward in this awkward position any more than a bird could fly with a sack tied to one foot.

They dropped below the clouds, spinning. The air cleared, leaving just a spray of rain. Edward looked down and saw the lights of a town below. Car headlights streamed along a highway. There was the gleam of a river. Then he was crashing through tree branches. His robe tore away completely, and he hit the ground with a splash and a thud, as the Ghastly Horror let go of him and vanished, dissolving into the air.

"Edwaaarddd!" it shrieked his name one last time.

He lay still in the dark and the rain, face down in mud. He rolled onto his side so he could breathe, coughing, and for a moment he just lay there, too stunned to move, amazed to be alive.

He reached up and fingered the dragon scale around his neck, remembering how Dr. Basileus had said it might protect him sooner than anyone expected.

Even Dr. Basileus couldn't have expected this.

He raised himself up on one elbow. That was painful, but his arm wasn't broken. He'd banged the elbow, either falling through the trees or tumbling down the stairs back home. He hurt all over, but as he sat up he realized that, for all he doubtless had a lot of scratches and bruises, he wasn't seriously injured.

He staggered to his feet and looked up. The remains of his robe flapped from a branch high overheard, like an abandoned parachute.

He was in a park of some sort, and could only think to find his way out of it. He discovered a path, but the gravel hurt his bare feet, so he followed it on the grass until he came to low brick wall. There must have been a gate around somewhere, but he didn't see it.

With difficulty, he heaved himself over the wall, landing with an *oomph!* in a flower bed on the other side.

There were shops on the street facing him, most of them closed, but some restaurants and a drugstore were open. A few cars drifted by, and two or three pedestrians, leaning into the light rain with umbrellas.

As Edward started walking, he realized he was not in any immediate danger just now, but in a very difficult predicament. People were starting to stare. One of the motorists slowed down and called out to him, "Are you all right, son?" but Edward said nothing and kept on walking.

Here he was on a chilly night in the middle of a town he did not know, shivering, splattered with mud, wearing just an old pair of swimming trunks which had, worse yet, ripped right up the middle seam.

He had no way of getting home. How could he possibly explain how he'd gotten there and expect anyone to believe or help him? That was the problem with magical experiences, he was beginning to realize. If you suddenly drop into the normal world, people just can't cope.

Well, I live in this magical house which is also a dragon. I'm not really sure where it is but it's on a hilltop which is also part of the dragon, and I was swimming inside the walls before a winged monster grabbed me and dropped me off here.

Yeah, right, kid. Tell me another story.

He was too tired and bewildered to move, much less to think up a more plausible excuse for his condition. The fall had knocked the wind out of him. He just sat down on curb, and huddled tight, his hands around his legs, his face against his knees, and shivered, waiting for something to happen.

It wasn't long before a car came to a stop in front of him. He looked up wearily and saw a flashing light. A police car. Someone put a warm jacket around him and helped him up and into the car.

The policeman drove and said nothing. His radio crackled. Once or twice he picked up a speaker and replied into it. Edward couldn't make out most of the policeman's words, though he might have said, "Tell them that I've got him," which didn't quite sound like something a policeman ought to say.

Tell who? Edward didn't know.

He was feeling light-headed and weak. He only wanted to lie down on the back seat of the car and let the rocking motion put him to sleep. He loosened his seatbelt and slid down onto the seat. The policeman did not respond. Edward lay there and he could see by the flashes from passing streetlights that he actually did have a couple of nasty-looking cuts on his legs and deep scratches across his chest, either from falling through branches or from the monster's claws. He touched the ugliest spot on his right leg. It hurt to do so. He saw that he had blood on his finger.

He wasn't worried about that. Surely the policeman would take him to the hospital and they'd bandage him and he'd be okay. At worst he might need a few stitches. More than anything else, he wanted a warm bath and then to be allowed to go to bed, where he could hide under the covers and pretend that none of this had happened.

That would be better than trying to explain. He was in trouble and he knew it. They'd just moved in to the new house and he realized that he didn't even know the phone number. He wasn't sure there *was* a phone number. He tried to remember the number of his mother's cell phone, but couldn't.

He was just too woozy.

They'd check him out at the hospital.

But somehow he didn't end up in a hospital. That was wrong. He knew it was wrong. He couldn't focus on precisely why it was wrong, but he was certain.

There were things he couldn't remember. Possibly he had been unconscious for a while. He only knew that he somehow found himself sitting at a table in the middle of a cold, concrete room, under bright lights, still soaking wet, in his ripped trunks and nothing else, looking like a mud-splattered, bloody mess.

"What is your name?" someone demanded.

The woman seated across from him was older than his mother, her hair silver. She had on something like a military uniform, but black. Presumably she was some sort of social worker or policewoman, even if she did wear a silver skull-and-crossbones on her lapel.

Her manner wasn't very reassuring either.

"Your *name*. You do have a name, don't you?"

"It's Edward."

"Edward what?"

"Just Edward."

The woman paused, and took some notes on a little pad.

Edward really did not want to talk to her, or anybody while he was like this. Not only was he cold and wet, but he'd always been shy about being undressed in front of strangers, even a doctor. He was beginning to realize how much the right clothing makes you feel confident. If you have to face a ferocious tiger, would you rather do it in just a pair of ripped swimming trunks, or wearing denim and army boots? The tiger will probably get you anyway, but the choice is obvious.

"Please," he said, hugging his sides and banging his knees together, "can I have something to wear?"

The woman snapped her fingers. A man wearing a similar black uniform brought Edward an orange jumpsuit. He even offered him a towel, but made no effort to help as Edward got up unsteadily and dried and cleaned himself as best he could. He had a lot of bruises. The gash on his right thigh looked pretty bad, although it wasn't bleeding. He wanted to see a doctor about it. He didn't understand why no one had taken him to see a doctor.

Nevertheless, he felt a lot better when he put on the jumpsuit. He had to roll up the cuffs and the sleeves, but it would do.

He sat down again, stiffly.

"Edward, you must tell me what I need to know. We'll be here all night if you don't."

Maybe he was just lightheaded, still in shock, but he felt a bit defiant.

"You tell me what your name is first," he said.

The woman pursed her lips, then said, "You may call me Mrs.

Morgentod."

Edward paused. He was beginning to be really afraid again. *You may call me* is not the same as—nor as friendly as—*my name is*. And *Morgentod?* He was good at languages, and starting to study them in school. He knew a few words of German. *Those* words. *Morgen* means *morning*. *Tod*, pronounced like "toad," means dead or death. Mrs. Morning-Death or Mrs. Dead-by-Morning?

He was starting to wonder how he was going to get out of here.

Mrs. Morgentod smiled sweetly, the same way, he imagined, a cobra does right before it eats its victim. He drew back from her. His chair scraped.

"Edward," she said gently. "You have to tell me. Who are you? I want to help you. You were in quite a state when you were found. *Who did this to you?"*

He realized now that he had to be very careful, or else he would get his parents in trouble. He'd heard of such things, and of how children sometimes get taken away from their parents and put in foster homes, which was usually a bad thing. Besides, he loved his parents, and he didn't even dislike his sister. He wanted to go home, to be with them.

But he had no possible explanation.

"I fell," he said.

That wasn't a lie. He had.

Mrs. Morgentod changed the subject.

"Are you hungry, Edward?"

He realized that he was actually famished. He hadn't eaten since breakfast.

He nodded.

Mrs. Morgentod snapped her fingers again and the same attendant came in and set down a tray in front of Edward, on which were a cup of soda, a hamburger wrapped in foil, and a packet of french fries.

Edward sipped the soda (which was lukewarm, its ice having melted), nibbled a few fries (which were cold), and took a couple bites out of the hamburger (which didn't taste right either).

Suddenly Mrs. Morgentod said something very startling indeed.

"Edward, what do you know about dragons?"

He dropped the hamburger onto the tray.

"Tell me, Edward, about dragons?"

"What about them?"

"Tell me what you know."

"You mean, like, dinosaurs?"

"Dragons, Edward. It is time for the evasions to end. Tell me what you know about dragons and you won't suffer…very much. I might even find a place for you, in the new order of things, if you are willing to work for us."

Edward put his fingers to the golden dragon scale he wore around his neck.

"Who's 'us'?" he said.

Mrs. Morgentod's eyes widened. She screamed at him. "Take that off *right now!"*

"No!" he said. "I won't."

She snapped her fingers yet again and this time the attendant came in with a pair of wire-cutters.

Edward ducked under the table as the man came for him, then managed to escape Mrs. Morgentod's grasp. They chased him around the table. He did his best to keep it between them and himself. When Mrs. Morgentod closed in from his right and the attendant from his left, he ducked under the table again, then flipped it up at them and ran for the door.

He pulled the door open and saw that the corridors outside were made of stone and lit with torches. There was a man in what looked like armor, carrying a torch, coming toward him up the left-hand corridor.

He turned back to face Mrs. Morgentod and the assistant.

"This isn't a police station, is it?" he said, not really expecting an answer.

Both glared at him, and *hissed,* not as a human being would, but more as a crocodile might. Indeed, their faces seemed to change shape, to bulge outward and become distinctly lizard-like, with long, sharp teeth. But he didn't stick around the watch. He had only a glimpse of them—and of the hamburger, which had sprouted legs and was scurrying across the floor—before he ran as fast as he could down the right-hand corridor.

His feet slapped on cold, rough stone and, as he ran, he could feel that this place, like his own house, was also *alive,* but very different.

He could not sink into the walls or floor. This place rejected him. It *hated* him, for all it clearly knew he was there.

Wherever he ran, the torches in the walls extinguished themselves, leaving him groping in darkness. As he touched the walls, they too were *hostile* in a way he could not quite define. The sensation was like an electrical shock.

Footsteps clattered behind him. Torches floated in the darkness, drawing nearer. He ran, gasping for breath. His right leg hurt terribly. He knew he'd torn it open again and was bleeding, but there was no time to do anything about it.

The very walls tried to trap him. He felt the stones grinding, actually closing in, but when he clutched the dragon-scale he wore and squeezed hard, somehow the hostile forces could not actually touch him.

He burst through a pair of large double doors into a brightly-lit room and skidded across the floor, bumping into a large, book-covered table before he realized what a bad mistake he'd made.

Dozens of people in black uniforms looked up at him sternly. Some of them had the lamprey mouths of Ghastly Horrors.

Those that had been seated rose. All of them closed in on Edward as he backed away out of the room, onto a balcony of sorts, and against a railing.

It was shock to realize where he was. There was a steering wheel, like a ship's wheel, set in the middle of the floor. Beyond the railing, two hemispheres of glass, enormous observatory windows, bulged into the night. He looked quickly down over the railing and was unsurprised to see cannons on the lower level.

He was in *another* dragon house, the house of the enemy, the Forces of Darkness, or whatever they were supposed to be called.

He was trapped.

"Edward," said Mrs. Morgentod, whose face was now very crocodile-like. "Give up. You aren't going anywhere."

She seemed to be the enemy leader. Her henchmen and assorted horrors filled the doorway. Off to his right there was a stair, just like in his own house. Men with torches, in black armor, came to the top of the stairs and waited.

He looked over the railing again. He seriously considered jumping. Instead he squeezed on the golden dragon scale and tried to send out a mental message, though he didn't know how to do it: *Somebody. Please help me. I'm here. Come quick!*

What happened next came almost too quickly for him to follow.

One of the observatory windows exploded inward, and there was something, huge and dark flapping through the air toward him.

The men in the black uniforms yanked out pistols and started shooting. The Ghastly Horrors sprouted wings and leapt into the air, in a whirlwind of confusion, battling something, as claws slashed and wings fluttered and bits of Ghastly Horrors splattered all over the windows and onto the balcony deck. Something splashed into Edward's face that smelled like a mixture of sewage and dirty motor oil.

He sputtered and tried to wipe the stuff out of his eyes with his sleeve. Half blinded, he nearly fell over the railing, and was clinging on desperately when he heard a voice calling out, "Edward! Come to me now! Edward!"

He saw arms stretched out for him, and he deliberately rolled over the railing and let himself fall.

Something hard and cold caught him, and in an instant, with a thunder of wings, he was carried through the broken window, out into the night air, up, up, faster, and faster, until all sounds of pursuit and gunfire had faded away behind, and he was soaring over cloud cover, beneath brilliant stars.

It took him several minutes to sort things out. What held him in its arms now—gently, the way a parent would carry a child—was made of living stone, but he *knew* this stone by feel. This was the stone of his *own* house for which he had, as Doctor Basileus had phrased it, *an affinity*.

More than that, it almost felt as if it were a part of him, flesh of his flesh.

Huge stone wings tore through the air with tremendous force, sufficient to keep even such a heavy thing aloft.

He had been rescued by one of the gargoyles, like the one he and Margaret had found in the woods on the day of the picnic.

He looked up into its stone face, which was sharp-eyed and fierce, with a hooked nose and horns, but somehow it seemed to be a *good* face, one you could rely on.

"Do you have a name?" he asked after a while.

"I am called Gargoyle."

"I mean, a shorter name?" Edward felt himself drifting off to sleep again, from relief and sheer exhaustion. He couldn't think clearly. He was starting to get silly. He thought of the phrase "punch drunk" but couldn't define it. "May I call you Gargy? Gargle...?"

"You may *not*. I have my dignity. All of my kind do. Just Gargoyle."

"Then how do you tell yourselves apart?"

"Each one of us pronounces it differently, but in ways no human ear, even yours, can distinguish."

"Oh," said Edward. For all he was several thousand feet in the air, in the arms of a winged stone-man, he hadn't felt this safe in a long while.

He closed his eyes, and barely heard Gargoyle say, "Rest now. You are needed back at the house. It is most urgent. Things are not going well."

Chapter Seven
Haunted House

Gargoyle gently shook Edward awake. They were descending now, out of dark clouds. Edward turned in the creature's arms and looked down. He could make out the house, the driveway, and the family SUV sitting there, but only dimly. The house lights were out. The storm had started up again, wind whipping the trees around. Rain sprayed into his face like surf.

Nevertheless he could tell that the darkened house had somehow *changed.* It looked less like a house and more like a ridgeline, rough and irregular, or maybe more like the scaled and spiked back of an enormous dragon.

Gargoyle dropped rapidly, wings thundering, and then hovered just outside the smashed window and gaping hole where Edward had been snatched out of his own bedroom.

The stone arms gently placed him inside.

"Edward," the creature said. "Now all hope is with you." It began to flutter away slowly into the darkness.

"But, aren't you going to help me?"

"Yes, but I have tasks elsewhere. Now go!"

And the Gargoyle was gone. Edward stood alone in the dark, inside his own bedroom, the wind and the rain whipping around him, and he stepped forward very gingerly as he realized he was walking barefoot on broken glass, splintered wood, and bits of stone.

He groped around until he found his dresser, then slid his hand into a drawer for the flashlight he kept there.

He snapped the flashlight on, and immediately gasped, aloud, "Oh, *no*—"

His bookshelf and his "museum" were smashed, everything dumped onto the floor. He crouched down and tried to gather things back together. Fortunately the rain hadn't gotten this far, only a little spray; but he couldn't exactly wipe anything dry on his jumpsuit. He was soaking wet. All he could think to do was push everything under the bed, where the books would be a little bit protected.

It was just as he discovered his precious Fokker Triplane smashed, its upper wing and landing gear broken off, that suddenly a light shone right at him and he heard his name called out.

"Edward! Thank God—!"

The light dazzled him. He crouched there, holding up the Triplane, and all he could think to say was, "It's broken," as if that somehow explained a great deal more in some manner he could not quite put into words.

"Edward!" It was Margaret, holding a flashlight a lot stronger than his.

"Mags?"

She hauled him to his feet and hugged him.

"Edward! I thought you were dead! They got Mom! I think they got Dad too!"

He felt the airplane crunch between them. Somehow that still mattered to him in a way he couldn't define. He pushed away from her, gathered up the pieces, or as many as he could find, and put them in his dresser. While he was there, he started rummaging through the other drawers.

"Edward! Are you all right?"

He realized he'd probably hit his head, and maybe he wasn't thinking all that clearly.

"I fell," he said, and went on rummaging through the drawer.

From deep within the house, something howled, like a screeching trumpet.

"We can't stay here! We have to get away!" She pulled on his arm.

Maybe it was her own fear that actually did clear his head. He had never seen his sister like this, her hair a mess, her eyes wide, close to tears.

"I know where we can go," he said.

He held a bundle of dry clothes under one arm. He stuffed his own flashlight in the pocket of his jumpsuit and relied on his sister to light their way. He touched the doorknob of the door that looked like a closet, and for a moment it was as if he could *feel* what was beyond it, and it was only because *he* was there that the house reshaped itself and a stairway appeared in what would have otherwise been a closet.

He opened the door. Mags pointed her flashlight, revealing a stairway. The screeching sound from elsewhere in the house seemed to be getting closer. There was no time to lose.

They hurried into the stairwell and closed the door behind them.

"I found this when I went exploring," he said.

He led the way, Margaret following with her flashlight in hand, Edward's shadow cast huge before them.

Something thumped against the door behind them and rattled the knob, but didn't seem to know how to open it.

They hurried on. The wooden stairs beneath Edward's feet felt like no more than wood, cold, smooth, dry. If the house was still *alive*, it was somehow withdrawn from him. He could barely feel its *pulse*, if that was the right word. Something was very wrong.

He came to another door, opened it, and got out his own flashlight, directing the beam around the old-fashioned, dusty bedroom he'd found before. All was as he'd remembered it, the bed that didn't look like it had been slept in for a hundred years, the ancient framed pictures, the nightstand, the closets with old-fashioned women's clothing on the hangers.

It was like he imagined his great-grandmother's room must have been like. Somehow he knew it was a friendly place. They'd be safe here for a while at least. When he touched the wall here, indeed, it seemed a little more alive. The wallpaper rippled, or maybe it was a trick of the light. He wasn't sure. Now that he thought himself safe, even for the moment, he was able to let go, and all the weariness and hurt of the night's adventures caught up with him. He tried to make it to the bed, but fell to his knees halfway there, then dropped to the floor, onto all fours. His flashlight rolled away.

"Edward! Are you hurt."

"A little bit."

She helped him onto the bed, and when he winced and yelped she was suddenly in charge, all business. She got him out of the jumpsuit. He yelped again when she did because the wound on his right leg had become stuck to the cloth.

Margaret made an "Ew" sound when she saw what condition he was in, but did not hesitate. There was a bathroom adjoining the bedroom. She went in. He heard water running. Then she came out with a hot, wet towel and wiped where he was hurt. Then she came back again with a bottle of alcohol and another towel. Before long she had him cleaned and bandaged, and he managed to make it into the bathroom by himself and change out of his ruined swimming trunks into some of the clothes he'd brought with him, proper underwear, blue jeans and a t-shirt and a sweatshirt. He realized he'd only managed to grab one flip-flop sandal, which wasn't going to do him any good. No matter. He limped back into the bedroom—his leg was getting stiff—and flopped down onto the bed, sending up a cloud of dust.

He coughed, and lay there as Margaret rearranged him a bit and rolled him under the covers. Then she lay down beside him, on top of the covers, her flashlight still in her hand, shining it over the walls and ceiling as if she were looking for something. Edward could tell how tense she was. She was really scared, despite putting up a brave front.

Far away, things howled and thumped throughout the house. Once in a while Edward could hear something fall and crash.

"I don't think they can get us," he said.

"Why not?"

"Because of this." He showed her the King Dragon scale he wore around his neck.

"What's that?"

He tried to explain, but his words came out all jumbled, and then after a while he stopped explaining, and drifted off into exhausted sleep.

His dreams, surprisingly, were not entirely unpleasant. There were monsters in the darkness, for sure, but there was also a comforting presence closer at hand. Once before he fell asleep, or perhaps a little after, he thought he saw, in the circle of light from his sister's flashlight, a face appear in the wallpaper, as if pressing through from the other side.

He wasn't afraid of it. The face seemed to be saying, "You can stay in my room as long as you need to. It's all right."

* * * *

When he awoke the next morning, the room was still in semi-darkness. It was a dark room under any circumstances, without any outside windows, just a couple skylights overhead.

Margaret had lit an oil lamp on the nightstand by the bed. She was seated at the makeup table, examining the numerous bottles and jars.

He sat up.

"Mags?"

She turned around.

"Edward, are you all right?"

He shifted painfully, and sat cross-legged. "A little stiff," he said. He supposed that after being snatched, squeezed, clawed, shaken, swung, dropped through trees, and sent body-surfing down a lightning-bolt, this was to be expected.

She was just nervously fidgeting with the bottles on the makeup table. She was still scared.

"What do we do now?" she said.

"Find some breakfast?" He actually was famished, not having eaten anything since yesterday's breakfast but for a couple limp french fries and one bite of highly doubtful hamburger.

"Edward!" She angrily threw one of the bottles to the floor. "Don't be stupid! I mean, what do we do about finding Mom and Dad, and about...*them!* All you can think about is your stomach!"

As if on cue, his stomach rumbled.

"I suppose I should try to explain. How much do you know?"

"About what?"

He spread out his hands. "About everything."

"I only know that yesterday I was in my room with the computer on the windowsill, going through My Space, when suddenly a bunch of those *things* came in through the window—"

"They're called Ghastly Horrors, genus *Ghastus*, species *Horribilus*—"

"Do you have any idea what it's like when one of those things *screams* right in your face? It's like a really loud air raid siren going off inside your head, and you can't move, and you probably fall to the floor like you're dead and have a nosebleed. I know I did. They could have eaten me if they wanted to, but they didn't seem interested. They just poured in through the window, hundreds of them. I don't think they were after me. They were after Mom and Dad and after *you,* Edward—"

"Yeah, they found me."

"I'm not sure what happened after that. Everything went crazy. The house was dark. I called out for Mom and Dad, but I only heard the *things* laughing. A lot later I heard your voice and came and found you in your room. You looked really beat up, and a little crazy yourself. You were wearing this—"

She picked up his blood-and-mud-and-worse-splattered orange jumpsuit from off the floor. He noticed for the first time that it had large black lettering on it, arranged in an arc, reading: DEPARTMENT OF EVIL. Below that, in smaller type, in a straight line, was the word JANITOR.

She threw it away in disgust.

He tried to tell her some of the things he had learned.

After a while she just waved her hand. "This is all too weird, Edward. Dragons, monsters, wizards, a guy from outer space named—"

"Zarcon of Zarconax—"

"—it's too much. Okay. I quit. I think I'll just go insane now."

"But you *can't!*"

"And why not?"

Now he was the one who was afraid. He felt himself almost about to cry, which was not something he wanted to do in front of his big sister.

"Because I need you," he said softly.

Then he thought it best to change the subject, quickly. He moved to the edge of the bed, rolled up his bluejeans to his knees, and then carefully pressed his bare feet *into* the floor, ankle deep. Then he stood up and sank down a little further, as if wading in something thick as molasses.

"I bet you can't do this."

She tried to press her own right foot through the floor. She was wearing sneakers. She made a tapping sound on the wooden floorboards. Then she seemed to get the idea and pulled off one shoe and one sock. She stood up and pushed her foot against the floor. But it wouldn't go through.

Meanwhile, he walked back and forth, and the floorboards rippled like water.

"This is just too weird," she said, backing away.

"I have an *affinity,* Doctor Basileus said."

"Doctor who?"

"Not the guy on television. Doctor Basileus. I think he's supposed to be my teacher. He and Zarcon came to visit Dad in that blimp thing that's anchored to the roof. Didn't you notice that?"

She sat down again and put her sock and shoe back on.

"No," she said, very slowly, and deliberately, "I did *not* have time to notice a *blimp* anchored to the roof, *nor* did I get to meet any strange doctors, *much less* a robot insect-man from another planet called, called—"

"Zarcon of Zarconax. He said everybody there has the same name, Zarcon, only each one pronounces it slightly differently—"

"Okay if I go nuts now? My brother's wading in the floor, which is impossible. La-la! Lose my mind!" She was rocking back and forth, beginning to sob.

He reached out to steady her.

"Please don't."

"Okay," she said slowly. "But what are we going to *do?*"

"I think we have to get used to things being really weird for a while. That's the first thing."

"And then?"

"Watch this."

He pulled off his sweatshirt and the t-shirt underneath and tossed them onto the bed. Then he crouched down, hands folded, arms out, covering his ears, the way they did it in swim class, and dove through the floor.

"Edward!" his sister screamed, but he could hardly hear her.

It was like a bellyflop again, and harder to get through. He had to concentrate, to deliberately think himself through the "surface" of the floor, and stroke with his arms and drag the lower half of his body through, because he wasn't wearing just skimpy swimming trunks this time, but bluejeans and a belt. Nevertheless, there was the same popping sensation, as if a membrane had given way, and then he was tumbling head over heels in an almost liquid darkness, but a little colder than before, and less pleasant to the touch. There came the same rush of sensation as the first time he'd done this, as if he could reach for miles and see in a dozen directions at once. He felt everything, as if the entire house and even the ridge beyond it were part of his own body, but now there was something different, something he did not like.

THE DRAGON HOUSE | 73

It almost felt as if he were covered with scabs, and were being bitten by mosquitos. He was aware of bad things, invaders, all over the house and moving through it. He could see the Ghastly Horrors slithering through hallways and rooms. Some of them had affixed themselves to walls and ceilings, attached by their toothy, circular mouths, like lampreys sucking the blood of a gigantic fish.

He steadied himself, floating in the darkness, then swam back toward the room he'd just left. He pressed his face forward, until the wallpaper stretched out in the shape of his face and he could shout, "Hey Mags! Look at me!"

But she didn't hear him. She was down on her knees running her hands over the floor where he'd disappeared.

He drifted back. Down below, was only darkness. He could still feel the presence of intelligence there, the mind of the house, the dragon itself, but it seemed far away, and he couldn't see it, as if a dark cloud were blocking his vision.

He swam upward, toward a light. As he neared it, the darkness around him grew warmer and more pleasant, the scabby, pin-pricking sensations fading away.

He bobbed up into a room suffused with a faint, golden light. Someone caught him under the arms and hauled him up out of the floor. The touch was warm and dry and firm.

He turned around and found himself face-to-face with an old woman in an old-fashioned dress and her hair up in a bun, looking like everybody's stereotypical grandmother.

His first impulse was to try to cover his bare chest with his hands, but she slapped them away and said, "Don't be silly. I know what boys look like. Do you think I've never been to a beach?"

She smiled sweetly, then took him by the shoulders, led him over to a chair in front of a makeup table, and sat him down. He realized that he was in a room absolutely like the one he had just left, down to the last detail, save that there was no Department of Evil jumpsuit bunched up on the floor and no sign of Margaret.

"It's still my room," she said, "as long as I am here to remember it."

"I don't understand," said Edward.

"Not that you should expect to understand everything right away. That comes with time, with many years of practice, and still it all seems a muddle sometimes. But—excuse me, I have been impolite. Introductions are in order. You must be Edward."

"Uh-huh."

"I am Miss Armitage, but that sounds a little too formal so you may call me Miss Emily. Perhaps you have heard of my more famous brother, Henry, who was a professor at a little college in Massachusetts."

"No…?"

"Probably not, dear. But you would have liked him. He was very good at dealing with horrors. There was a particularly nasty one in Dunwich back in the nineteen twenties, and he put it down right smartly. He would have been able to teach you quite a lot."

"I don't suppose I could ever meet him?"

"Sadly, no. He has long since passed on. He'd be…let me see…about a hundred and sixty if he were alive today."

"And you?"

"What about me, dear?"

"Are you a…a ghost?"

She reached out and touched Edward on the bare shoulder. She felt solid enough. Her hand was dry and cool. A typical old-lady's touch.

"I'm not really sure, Edward. I am like you. I am part of the house."

Edward drew back from her.

"But this is crazy. I'm *alive.*"

He hugged his own shoulders to reassure himself that he was made out of skin and muscle, not wood.

"Nevertheless, Edward, when I first came here, I learned I had the same affinity to the house that you do. I could swim through the house as you do, though it was a little harder for me at first, because girls in those days were expected to be modest. Most of the time I would just daintily slip a hand through the wall, and that would have to do. I was mistress of the Dragon House, Edward, even as you are to be my successor, and its master."

"I don't feel like I'm master of anything just now."

"No, and it's more of a partnership, a *kinship* perhaps, anyway, because, as you probably know, the dragon has a mind of its own. You will learn all this, in time."

"But why am I here?" said Edward. "Why didn't you just stay on the job?"

She sat down on the bed, and for a while said nothing, as if her mind were elsewhere. She even sniffled a little bit, and dried a tear with a hankie.

"It's hard to explain, Edward. I came here a very long time ago. Everyone I knew is long gone. It's hard to think about it all sometimes. I may well be dead, and my soul may well have gone on to its reward years ago. I was even older than my brother, you know. Our first mother died, and our father married again, to a woman much younger than himself. The famous Henry Armitage was the baby of the family. I was grown up before he was even born. So, if you add all that up, I could very well be dead, and not really a ghost, but more like a pattern left behind in fabric of the house, a recording that's being played for you now. It's very confusing sometimes."

"But you're here..." Edward wanted to complete that sentence with *in the flesh* or *you seem really alive to me,* but it just trailed off.

"I'm here, and I am supposed to help you, Edward, particularly with the difficult situation that has come up. The house has been taken over by the enemy. Unless you regain control and drive them out, they will turn the dragon and all its quite awesome powers over to the cause of evil. I know that you are unprepared for this task. As the others have told you, this has all happened much too quickly, before you could be trained. But nevertheless, you must rise to the occasion and become a *hero,* Edward, or all is lost."

"And if that happens?"

"If this particular dragon goes over to the forces of darkness, then, very likely, the balance tips irretrievably, and evil wins. If that happens, things will go very uncomfortably for you, for your sister, and for your parents."

Margaret. He had forgotten about her. She'd been close enough to panic already, and he was sure his disappearing through the floor and being gone for a long time wasn't going to help.

"I'd better get back," he said.

"Yes, you had. And, Edward, don't go into the walls frivolously like this. When you do, the enemy can feel your presence. They can reach you, in the dark. Don't do it unless you absolutely have to, until all of this trouble is over. Promise?"

"Okay," said Edward.

Then Miss Emily motioned him to get up and face the wall.

"But this time you have to," she said. Before he could react, she put her hands on his shoulders and shoved him through.

He tumbled in darkness again, and righted himself, floating in what felt like a thick, almost oily fluid. This wasn't fun at all. It was more like being immersed in dirty oil, although he could breathe, and he could feel the whole house as an extension of himself; but it was almost as if he were paralyzed, lying helpless in a huge, useless body slowly growing numb all around him.

Something moved down below. He thought first of wriggling snakes, piled on top of one another, but then of a school of sharks, rising toward him.

He started swimming. He shouted out "Mags! Mags! Where are you?" and after a moment he heard his sister calling his name and pounding on a wall. He swam toward the sound and suddenly burst through, not a wall, but a ceiling. Up and down had gotten confused somehow.

He hung down from the ceiling over the bed, stuck as if his belt-buckle had gotten caught on a nail.

Something brushed against his feet. He kicked frantically.

"Mags! Pull me through!"

She was at the other side of the room, pounding on the wall, but she heard him and came over, caught him by both wrists, and yanked him down onto the bed, where he landed with a bounce and a flop.

"Okay, okay," Margaret said. "I'm convinced. You're special. *Now* what?"

Edward got off the bed, wincing a bit because his leg still hurt. He put on his t-shirt and sweatshirt and rolled his pants cuffs down to his ankles.

"First breakfast," he said, "then we save our parents, then we save the universe."

"Fine," said Margaret. "In that order."

"Great."

"Simple as that."

But it did not seem simple at all when, very cautiously, he opened the door and looked down the stairs up which they had fled last night.

He knew the Horrors had been there, and they had left traces.

THE DRAGON HOUSE | 77

There was a gray, unpleasant mass all over the stairs and walls and hanging down from the ceiling. He thought of the way that wasps or termites chew up wood and mix it with their saliva and then spit it out to form a kind of plaster, out of which they build their nests. Something like that had been splattered all over the inside of the stairwell. It had a texture like thin, brittle plastic, or maybe like asbestos, dusty and gritty and sharp, very nasty stuff to be wading through in bare feet.

After just a few steps, he pushed Margaret back into the room.

"What do we do now?" she said.

"I don't know."

"Here you go, dear. I almost forgot," said another voice. It was Miss Emily, her face pressing through the wall of the room, her hand emerging holding out a pair of pink, fluffy slippers. "I wish I had something more appropriate, but you're not a very big boy, so these should fit."

The slippers dropped to the floor and she withdrew into the wall and was gone.

Edward looked at his sister and said, "I'll explain later."

"You don't have to," she said. "I'm going insane, remember?"

Ignoring this last remark, he put the slippers on, fully aware of how ridiculous he looked in them, but glad to have them. He was glad, too, that at least they did not have bunny-rabbit ears. Possibly in Miss Emily's day there were no such things as bunny-rabbit slippers.

Thankful for this small favor, he led Margaret down the stairs.

Chapter Eight
Runaway House

As they crunched their way down the stairs, Edward realized that he was completely cut off from the house. It was not merely that he was wearing the slippers and so couldn't feel anything beneath his feet, but that even when he reached out with a bare hand to steady himself—something he did reluctantly—he felt only the crumbling, gray stuff, not the house itself. He was sure he would not be able to pass a hand through these walls.

The walls were scabbed over.

The stairwell reminded him of imagery from TV commercials about the dangers of clogged arteries, about how goop made up of fat and bad cholesterol builds up inside and causes heart attacks in older people.

Fat, yes. The gray stuff had a texture of pork rind mixed with asbestos.

He imagined himself a blood cell inside a clogged artery.

Indeed, at the bottom of the stairs, the way was blocked entirely, just a solid mass of the awful stuff, which, fortunately, he and Margaret discovered simultaneously, would give way to a good, old-fashioned kick.

They broke through, exposing the door below, but the dust was hideous, and made them cough and gag and their eyes water.

The best either of them could do was pull their sweatshirts up over their noses, since they didn't have facemasks or even bandannas.

Edward tried to force the door open, but it wouldn't budge. Margaret, who was heavier and stronger, got it open, pushing with all her strength until it receded slowly into Edward's room, crunching and grinding.

They both squeezed through. Edward saw that everything in the room was covered with a thick, gray mass, and unless he wanted to come in here with pick and shovel, he wasn't going to be able to get anything out of his dresser or from under the bed, or anywhere. He would have to make do with what he had on, including the ridiculous, now uncomfortably dusty slippers, and what he had in his pockets (nothing, except a flashlight).

Despite the fact that he couldn't actually touch the house through the gray stuff, he could distinctly feel that the floor beneath his feet was shaking.

He looked at his sister and she at him.

Both of them seemed about to say, "Earthquake?" but both knew by now that the explanation could not be so mundane.

Edward made his way to what used to be the window, the hole in the wall through which the Ghastly Horror had burst out into the night with him in its clutches. The hole was smaller now, partially filled in with the gray stuff, as if, indeed, gigantic wasps spitting out chewed-up wood were intent on repairing the damage.

Nevertheless he could still see out. Margaret crowded beside him.

It took him a few minutes to make any sense out of what he was seeing.

He looked out over the vast array of rooftops and towers and gables of the house, and even as he watched these *changed,* windows vanishing like eyes drooping closed, towers and roofs shrinking down into less precise shapes, as if the whole house were retracting into itself, becoming less like a house and more like a series of cliffs, or just a natural hillside or ridgeline.

Or like the body of a dragon, it suddenly occurred to him.

And, beyond a certain point, there was something even stranger. Trees seemed to me *moving,* retreating in an orderly line away from him, but for a few nearer ones which inexplicably snapped and crashed and vanished.

If you're inside a moving train and you look into the far distance, mountains far away may not seem to be moving at all. Things a little closer shift slowly, those closer still do so quite a lot faster, until, if you look down at the railroad ties, they whiz by in a blur.

Nothing was whizzing by, but the landscape itself was shifting, slowly, but certainly, the woods beyond the far side of the driveway drifting past. He was sure. He watched one particularly large tree recede into the distance, passing from right to left.

The floor beneath his feet rumbled.

It wasn't the trees that were moving, he realized. It was the *house.*

"It's really alive," said Margaret in a low voice.

"Yes, it's alive. I told you that," said Edward. "But now it's *awake*. It's *crawling."*

"Where's it going?"

"I don't know. I don't think it's going to New Jersey. Or Ohio. Or New York. Or anyplace we'd ever *want* to go."

"Yeah," said Margaret, "I have a bad feeling about this, to coin a phrase."

"I don't think we should stay here," said Edward.

"Yeah."

Margaret opened the door to the hallway leading from the bedroom. This crackled and crunched a bit too, but the dust wasn't as bad.

The only problem was that just outside the door, one of the Ghastly Horrors hung like a sack, its suction-cup mouth affixed to the ceiling, its wings and limbs sagging limply beside it, but still wide enough to fill the entire hallway.

They stood there for a second, not knowing what to do, ready to slam the door shut, but nothing happened.

"I think it's asleep," said Margaret.

Edward knew better. He noticed how its throat slowly pulsed, as if it were swallowing continuously. It was *feeding,* like a leech or lamprey, sucking the vital energy out of the house itself.

There was nothing to do but get down onto the floor, into the dust and crackling gray stuff, and wriggle *under* the thing, which Edward managed to do, slowly, carefully, doing his utmost not to touch it or attract its attention.

On the other side he stood up, coughing. He wiped the dust off himself as best he could.

Margaret hesitated in the doorway.

"I'm bigger than you," she said. "I'm not sure if I can fit."

"You're going to have to."

Fearfully, she lay down on her back and wriggled slowly underneath, pausing in absolute terror every time she seemed about to *touch* the Horror.

"You can do it," he whispered.

She inched a bit more, but the great mass of the creature, hanging down, was just an inch or two above her. She lay still.

"I can't! I won't fit."

The Ghastly Horror shifted very slightly, dust falling from its wings.

"Quick," Edward said. "Just lie as flat as you can. Breathe out. Don't inhale. Pretend you're a deflated balloon. Then *give me your hands.*"

She did. He took her by the hands first, but when he realized that wouldn't do, by the wrists. She held on tightly to his wrists. Slowly, straining, trying very hard to be silent about it, he pulled her along the floor, under the sagging, black bulk, until she was clear, or almost clear, and she started to sit up.

That was when her foot accidentally scraped against the belly of the Horror.

Edward said nothing, but grimly pulled her away. Margaret let out a stifled moan.

The Horror fluttered its wings. It wriggled like a mass of jelly, even as Edward and Margaret backed away from it, moving down the hall.

But fortunately it did not fully awaken. It made a mewling sound, like some animal in the midst of a dream, but it remained where it was, attached to the ceiling.

Edward and Margaret edged away, into her room.

This wasn't much of an improvement. Her room, too, was filled with nasty gray stuff, and dust. Her laptop computer lay on the floor where it must have fallen when the Ghastly Horrors invaded the house through her open window.

The computer was still on. The screen glowed.

For a moment Edward thought this might be useful. Maybe they could look up *www.forcesofdarkness.com* and learn what the enemy was up to.

But then he noticed that something was oozing out of the keyboard, something that glistened like spit and moved like half-hardened glue. There was a great puddle of it on the floor, and it was *alive,* covered all over with little wriggling feelers.

It flowed toward them.

"That's the worst computer virus I've ever seen!" Margaret whispered. She pushed Edward back out into the hallway and pulled the door shut.

After a minute, the virus started oozing under the door. Margaret backed away.

Now they were caught between the Ghastly Horror hanging from the ceiling outside of Edward's room and this. In order to get to the top of the stairs that led down to the lower floors of the house, they'd have to squeeze around or under the Horror *again*, and that was not something Edward was ready to do. In just the few minutes they'd been watching it, it seemed to have grown *larger*.

The only way to go was over the bannister, performing one of those acrobatic tricks every child is strictly forbidden to attempt for fear of broken necks.

But there was no help for it. Edward, who had always been a good tree-climber, went first, lowering himself from the upper railing, onto the slanting, lower bannister. His feet slipped. The soles of the slippers he was wearing were completely smooth. For a moment he was left hanging there, while Margaret, above him, reached down to grab.

"No," he whispered. "I'm all right."

He kicked off the slippers and caught hold of the bannister with his toes. Here there was almost none of the gray stuff or dust. He could feel the wood of the house with the bare soles of his feet. It was still *alive*, slightly warm, slightly soft. For an instant he even had a sense of the dragon itself, far away and far below, much distracted, maybe hurt, but *aware* of him and trying to help.

Certainly his footing was a lot steadier. He was able to let go of the railing above with his right hand, then lean over, catch hold of the bannister, and lower himself onto the steps.

Margaret followed. She was wearing sneakers. Fortunately the rubber soles gave her just enough of a grip. He reached up to try to catch her if she fell, but she didn't fall. Her reach was longer. The drop wasn't as difficult for her.

He recovered his slippers and put them on again, first shaking out as much dust as he could. He and Margaret tiptoed slowly away. The Horror above them remained silent.

They made their way down a second flight of stairs, to the first floor. These were the front stairs of the house. The entranceway was right in front of them. It would be entirely possible, Edward realized, for them to just go out the front door, across the driveway, down the slope, and from there they could presumably jump down into the woods and the Dragon House would go lumbering on without them, no one the wiser.

And this would accomplish—what? It would leave Mom and Dad in whatever terrible danger they were in, Doctor Basileus and Zarcon of Zarconax to meet whatever dire fates *they* were enmeshed in, and, oh, by the way, it would mean the bad guys would win and very likely destroy the world, if not the entire universe.

So, Edward could have easily escaped out the front door, but he thought better of it.

Besides, he was getting really hungry. He hoped they could at least make it to the kitchen and find something to eat before the world had to end, if it came to that. It wasn't that he was a big eater—because he wasn't—but he hadn't eaten anything at all (but for a bite of that dubious hamburger later seen skittering away) in over twenty-four hours, and he might have had some rest, but he had still been through quite a lot, and he felt that if this went on much longer he was going to faint.

He swayed unsteadily and caught hold of Margaret's shoulder. Without saying anything, she put her arm around him and held him up.

They reached the kitchen without anything happening.

The kitchen, at least, seemed pretty much as it always had. Some cups and jars had fallen off shelves. There were a couple broken dishes on the floor. Even as Edward watched, a sugarbowl vibrated near the edge of the table. (He caught hold of it and put it back in the center.) The floor beneath their feet was clean tile.

Edward sat down. He felt the tabletop vibrating slightly with the movement of the house. He took his feet out of his slippers and touched the tile floor, and again he felt the house itself, alive, part of him yet distant, but he remembered what Miss Emily had said about not dropping through the floor or pushing through a wall unless he absolutely had to, so he just sat there and did nothing.

The electricity was off, but the contents of the refrigerator were still cold. Since it was morning, they had breakfast. Margaret got out milk and fruit, then a box of raisin bran, two bowls, and spoons.

They ate in silence for a while. Then she said, "I'm not sure how often we'll be able to get back here. Maybe we should take some supplies."

"I wish we had a backpack," said Edward.

But they didn't, and had to make do with a shopping bag, paper inside double plastic bags so that it had handles. Margaret gathered into it a few apples, some lunch meat, half a loaf of bread, three or four bottles of soda, two cans of chili with pull-tops, and a pack of cookies.

Then she took down the biggest steak knife there was from the holder on the wall.

"What's that for?" said Edward.

"In case we have to fight…you know what. Isn't that what we're supposed to do?"

"Supposed to?"

"We're the heroes. We go up against monsters."

"I don't think it works like that." Indeed, he knew it did not. This was not like that stupid *Narnia* movie he'd seen, in which they put a hundred-pound kid inside a suit of armor and gave him a sword and sent him into battle against five-hundred-pound ogres as if everybody were playing a game. No, he knew that if you try that all you're going to get is a red smear across the landscape with a few lumpy bits where the armor used to be. And he and Margaret didn't even *have* armor.

Nevertheless, she insisted on the steak knife. There was no scabbard, so she wrapped it in a towel and then slid it under her belt.

"Now what?" she said.

"I think we have to get upstairs, to the library."

"Back up *those* stairs?"

"I think a house this big has more than one way to get anywhere."

It was strange, of course, that they'd lived here almost a week and easily ninety percent of the house was still unexplored, and neither one of them really knew their way around.

But then, it had not been an ordinary week.

All they could do was try.

They found a stairway easily enough. It was in the far end of the kitchen, near the closet from which he had so unexpectedly emerged that first night in the house.

He wasn't sure this stairway had even been there before, but now a door hung open, and there it was. Edward got out his flashlight and shone it up the stairway. There was a lot of dust and some cobwebs, but none of the gray stuff.

"This should be okay," he said.

Nevertheless, Margaret, behind him, got out the steak knife, which she held in her right hand, hefting the bag of supplies in her left.

They ascended slowly and carefully. The steps vibrated slightly, and the walls trembled a little, but they made their way to the top without incident.

They emerged into a room Edward had never seen before, broad and open, like a ballroom, with large windows, pointed at the top like church windows, but closed with heavy drapes.

In the middle of the room was a department store mannikin, naked but for a top hat, with a flickering candle in one hand. With the other, it pointed off to the right.

Edward looked at it, then off to the right, and went in that direction, motioning for Margaret to follow.

She whispered to him, "There was a time, before I started going mad, when I would have said, 'That's really weird,' but, you know, nothing seems weird to me anymore."

"I know how you feel," Edward said.

They came to a large, arched doorway, leading into darkness. Edward shone his flashlight inside, and saw stacks of what appeared to be wooden boxes, piled as far as he could see. He didn't like the looks of this at all. It looked like a roomful of coffins.

"Are you *sure* this is the right way?" Margaret said.

"Well, that guy said—"

Edward looked back and saw that the mannikin with the candle was gone.

Margaret looked too, then shrugged and said, "No comment."

Nevertheless, Edward could think of nothing better to do than to proceed. He led Margaret into the room, which, indeed, seemed to be filled with coffins. It was dank and cold in there. The floor was muddy stone, as if they were deep inside the earth, inside a crypt. Now Edward was particularly glad for the slippers, although it still felt as if he were walking on ice.

He pointed his flashlight upward and breathed into the beam. He could see his breath.

"Let's get out of here," Margaret said.

"Good idea."

They walked faster. Something creaked. Something tapped. Then he was certain that something *inside* one of the coffins was rapping on wood, and this was taken up by another far ahead of him, and another off to the left, until it sounded like a forest full of woodpeckers. Something had clearly awakened and was sending messages to its fellows in the equivalent of Morse code.

They walked even faster, Margaret turning this way and that, her knife pointing, Edward's flashlight playing over the sides of the coffins.

"Walk steadily," Margaret said. "Don't run."

"Why not?"

"You don't want them to know we're afraid of them."

"But we *are* afraid of them," Edward said, lowering his voice.

"Yeah, I guess we are," said Margaret.

Just then a coffin lid creaked loudly, then crashed to the floor somewhere behind them, followed by the sound of something like a full garbage bag being dropped from an upper storey window, followed by teeth grinding together.

"I have a better idea," said Edward. *"Run!"*

Edward found it hard to do so in the slippers, which were by now heavy and coated with mud, but he managed a very rapid shuffle. Margaret, who had longer legs anyway, pulled ahead of him, just as he slipped and fell and rolled, still clinging desperately to the flashlight.

Margaret turned and came back for him. She had to clench the knife in her teeth while hauling him to his feet with her right hand and balancing the bag of groceries in her left.

Then they were running again. It was only after a while that Edward realized he'd lost the slippers and was running barefoot over cold, wet stones while something was trying to grab at his ankles. Behind them, something else dropped to the floor with a thud, which was rapidly followed by something else. They were being followed by thumping, squishing sounds.

Then there was a light up ahead.

"There!" Edward shouted, pointing.

They ran for it. The things behind them flopped and chittered. Edward didn't look back. He leapt into the air a couple times when something cold and rough made a serious attempt at his ankles.

Then they were through, into the light. It took his eyes a moment to adjust, and for his mind to make sense of anything, because they were moving now, the whole floor circling to the right. He was surrounded by poles, and wooden animals, and soft music was playing, and it took him a minute to realize where he was: in the carousel room, or one very much like it. He looked back the way they had come and saw that the dark doorway through which they emerged had snapped shut like a mouth. Then it was out of sight. Exhausted, he and Margaret clung to poles, and, before he quite realized what he was doing, Edward climbed aboard a wooden dragon that rose and fell and seemed to be more than wood, its eyes alive, its whiskers flowing in the wind. He looked back and saw that Margaret was riding something that looked half like a fish, half like a unicorn, and it, too, seemed to be alive.

They went around and around several times. The dark doorway, much to his relief, did not reappear, but for a while there was no other exit, and he wondered if they were stuck here, inside this enormous carousel, which seemed to change even as he rode on it, the wooden animals around him never quite the same if he looked at one, then looked away, then looked again.

Once he saw a tall, thin man in a top hat riding on what looked like the skeleton of a horse. Then he was gone, and there was only a wooden horse next to Edward, of the more conventional, painted sort.

He looked back. Margaret had somehow fallen behind. He could barely see her around the curve of the spinning floor.

He dismounted, and made his way back to her, steadying himself by grabbing one pole after another. He saw that she had managed to slip her knife back into the towel in her belt, and that she held onto the reins of her mount with one hand and held the bag of supplies in the other.

He took the bag from her.

"I think we have to get off," he said, starting to feel dizzy. "I don't know where we'll end up if we don't."

Without a word she dismounted and followed him. They made their way to the edge of the turning platform, and when they saw a lighted doorway approaching, they got ready, then jumped through.

Edward landed and rolled, then Margaret landed on top of him. He wriggled free, worried about that knife, but he saw that she had not hurt herself. The grocery bag had spilled. Together they retrieved cans, bottles, and an errant apple.

They stood in a half-lit hallway at the base of a spiral staircase. Edward started to climb, then hesitated, reluctant, when his bare foot touched the gray, crumbly stuff that Ghastly Horrors left behind. But there was no help for it. There was nowhere else to go.

He heard a faint voice crying from above, "Edward! Help me!"

He raced up the stairs, Margaret behind him, and found, on a landing halfway up, what he first took to be part of a broken machine. It looked like a toy, something triangular, made of greenish metal or plastic, an object the size of a very small TV or computer monitor, but with two distinct, oval eyes that he recognized. He also knew that chittering, insect-like mouth. One broken antenna wriggled forlornly.

"Zarcon...?" he said, picking up the object.

Margaret caught up with him. He turned to her and held up what he'd found.

"Mags, this is Zarcon. He's the alien I told you about."

But it wasn't Zarcon. It was just his head and a bit of neck. Nevertheless, Zarcon now seemed more composed than either Edward or Margaret.

"Greetings, young lady. You must be our brave Edward's sister, about whom I have heard so much—"

Margaret was still clearly having trouble making all this compute. She looked at Edward and said, "You know him—it—that?"

"I told you, this is—"

"Margaret Estelle Longstretch, daughter of Edward Charles Stuart Longstretch and Anastasia Marie Brahenski, now Longstretch, sister to Edward Eusebius Longstretch, I am indeed Zarcon, of the university of Zarconax in great metropolis of Zarconax on the planet Zarconax, in the solar system of Zarconax, in the cluster of Zarconax, in the galaxy of Zarconax—"

"Is *everything* called Zarconax?" Margaret interrupted.

"Yes, but we pronounce them differently."

THE DRAGON HOUSE | 89

Now even Edward was curious. "Is that the same galaxy as our own?"

"I don't know. You Earth people use different names for everything. It's so confusing."

"Let me guess," said Margaret, clearly about to go into her *Okay, I'll just lose my mind now* mode. "Everybody on your planet is named Zarcon, right?"

"Why of course. But…but…but…" He started sputtering and screeching, like the sound of a needle being dragged across a phonograph record. "Edw—Edw—ard—quick—hit the side of my head—knuckles—"

Edward rapped firmly.

"Ah, that's better," said Zarcon. "But, as I was about to attempt to impress upon you, upon you…in particular, is that while it may be pleasant to continue this amiable conversation and exchange ethnographic, linguistic, and astronomical information, there *is* a crisis that we must deal with."

"Yeah, I know," said Edward.

"Things are going very badly indeed, Edward."

"May I ask you just one more question?" Margaret said. "I really need to know."

"Yes, you may."

"Are you…a robot, or alive?"

"It is a meaningless distinction. On Zarconax, zarcon machines are made of flesh and wood and stone. We are able to grow and shape both living and unliving matter, incorporating both into ourselves as needed, until it becomes very difficult to distinguish the two, and there is no actual point in doing so."

Edward realized, for all that Margaret might not have, that there *was* a point here, something important, the distinction between the wood and stone of the house and the body of the living dragon, and between the dragon, the house, and *himself*. There were so many more questions *he* wanted to ask.

"But to the immediate matter at hand," said Zarcon of Zarconax.

"Yes," said Edward. "What happened to my parents, and to Doctor Basileus—and to the rest of *you?*"

"The last question I can definitely answer, which is to say that when we were surprised and overwhelmed by the Horrors, by the

Grues, by the Nightmare Things, one of them whacked my head off and kicked it down the stairs like a… I search for the phrase…"

"Like a football?"

"Very much so. After which, I am afraid, I was not able to witness much else that occurred. I am sorry, Edward, but I cannot answer your other questions."

"What do we do now?"

"That I can answer, or at least make suggestions. We proceed."

They made their way along a corridor thick with the gray stuff and occasionally blocked by it, Edward holding Zarcon in one hand and his flashlight in the other. He let Margaret do the kicking when they had to smash their way through, not merely because she was bigger and stronger but because she was wearing shoes. It was bad enough that Edward had to wade ankle-deep in the stuff, which felt like a combination of wood splinters and ground glass. He dearly wished he still had his slippers, or, better yet, a solid pair of knee-high riding boots.

Thick dust filled the air, swirling in the flashlight beam. He coughed hard and painfully. His eyes and nose ran.

Then, at last, the air seemed to clear a little, and once more he realized where he was, although it had looked very different the last time he had been here.

Now he was wading through piles of fallen books. They were in the library. Many of the shelves were smashed. Most of the books were on the floor. The whole room rolled and swayed slowly, like the cabin of a ship at sea.

A dimly glowing crystal skull lay in the midst of it all.

"Such disorder," the thing said. "How shall I ever put everything back in its proper place?"

Margaret stared at the skull, but refused to react.

"Friend Librarian is in a pitiful state," said Zarcon, "as am I."

"This mess…how shall I clean it all up?" said the librarian.

Edward wanted to suggest picking up the books one by one, but that seemed an almost cruel thing to say, so he kept quiet.

"And look at you, young man—you're a *mess!* Don't you know how to show some respect and clean up yourself before you come into a *library?"*

Edward realized that he was a mess, his bare feet almost black with mud and the gray stuff, one leg of his jeans soaked in mud from where he had fallen, his hands dirty. He could just imagine what his face looked like. Margaret looked pretty bedraggled, her hair completely wild and her cheeks smudged with sooty gray.

More immediately, the gash on his right thigh was hurting again and felt sticky. Very likely all the exertion had torn it open and he was bleeding once more. He probably needed stitches, but that was going to have to wait.

An odd thought came to him, and he had to ask Margaret, "How come Superman always has these incredible adventures without getting a hair out of place or a spot of dirt on his uniform?"

"You're not Superman," Margaret said. "Neither am I."

"I think he uses kryptonite hair gel."

"That wouldn't do him any good. Kryptonite would fry his brain."

Edward was again feeling a bit woozy as he paused to catch his breath. It occurred to him that if Margaret had the option of just going insane in difficult moments, maybe he should try it too. He ran a hand through his very messy hair, feeling grit and tangles, but no kryptonite goo. His brain felt fried nevertheless, as if it had been split open and sizzling in a pan for a couple days now.

"A mess," the skull moaned. "A mess. A mess."

"Sorry," he said.

"Clean it all up!"

"Actually, that gives me an idea," said Zarcon of Zarconax. "Edward, find the nearest maintenance closet."

"Where?"

"Yes, off to the side somewhere."

They found one, and opened it. Inside were various brooms, mops, an orange jumpsuit that Edward did not like the looks of hanging from a hook, and, on the floor, an old-fashioned vacuum cleaner, like a round barrel that moved on three wheels and had a hose sticking out of the front.

"Yes, yes, that is what we need," said Zarcon.

"We're going to *clean the place up?*"

"No, no. Not yet, anyway. Remove the top."

Margaret put down the bag of groceries she was still carrying and unscrewed the top of the vacuum cleaner and set it aside.

"Now put me in place."

Puzzled, Edward did what he thought Zarcon meant, and placed the alien's head, neck-first, into the open top of the vacuum cleaner.

Suddenly dozens of metal tendrils shot out from the neck, locking it into place, so that Zarcon was now joined to the body of the vacuum cleaner.

His eyes lit up. "Ah, yes! Much better!" He rolled forward slightly, trailing about three feet of cable and a two-pronged plug.

Edward picked up the end of the cable.

"Are we supposed to plug you in?"

"That won't be necessary, but thank you." Suddenly the vacuum cleaner's motor whirred, and the cable whipped out of Edward's hand, retracting into the round, metal body with a loud thwack.

Zarcon waved his two feet of hose in the air, his motor roaring even louder.

"And now, heroic Edward and brave sister Margaret, it is up to us to regain control of the Dragon House before it is too late. I am afraid all our other allies have been neutralized. It's just the three of us. But we shall prevail. Tally-ho!"

"Tally what?" Margaret asked.

"An old Earth expression. It means *get on with it.*"

Chapter Nine
The Skeleton House

"Maybe we *do* have to start with a little cleanup," Edward said.

"What do you mean?" said Margaret.

"Look at that."

She joined him in the doorway where he stood, looking from the smaller side room where they'd been into the main gallery of the library, and she saw what he saw.

The placed was *filled* with Ghastly Horrors. Edward gave up counting at two dozen, not just because they were so hideous to look at, but because, clustered together on the sides of the walls like bats in a cave, their shapes seemed somehow indeterminate, so that it wasn't easy to tell where one ended and another began.

They hung from the walls and from the ceiling and from the bookshelves. He could tell they were sucking the life out of the library, because even as he watched, the spines of the books on the nearest shelf started to fade and look old and dusty, their titles becoming illegible.

"The mess…" the librarian's crystal skull continued to complain, somewhere behind them.

"What do you have in mind, exactly?" Margaret asked.

Zarcon of Zarconax whirred his motor. "He has in mind…what he means is…young lady, you showed excellent foresight by bringing that cutting instrument…blade…"

"He means the steak knife," Edward whispered.

"Yes, exactly. The steak knife. Go now to the nearest of those things and cut it loose from the wall, the way you'd cut off a nasty growth you need to get rid of."

Margaret drew out the knife. "But won't it…? You mean *me?*"

Edward nodded. "He does."

She looked at the nearest horror, a bat-winged, black sack easily six feet long, hanging by its trumpet-shaped, sucker-mouth from a bookshelf. Even as they stood there, the books in that shelf started to collapse inward upon themselves, crumbling into mounds of dust.

"No..." moaned the librarian in the other room.

Margaret looked at the knife, then at the thing. She reached up, then drew away.

"What's the matter?"

"I can't do it." Her eyes were wide and she was breathing hard. Edward could tell she was genuinely afraid. She looked like she was going to use this as an excuse to go into the "I'll just go insane for a while" routine. After all, it was less than a week since she'd been an ordinary girl living an ordinary life in an ordinary Philadelphia neighborhood, and now she was being asked to dismember an unearthly monster with a steak knife. Yes, he could appreciate that she was under some strain.

"But someone's got to do it," he said.

She reached up again, then drew back.

"It's too high. I can't reach."

"Then lift me up."

She paused, then said, "Okay."

He took the knife from her and put one bare, grubby foot into her equally dirty palm. Neither of them said anything. He put his other foot in her other palm, and she lifted him without difficulty.

He held the knife in his teeth as he reached out with both hands to steady himself against the bookshelf, climbing as Margaret lifted him until he was standing on her shoulders.

Beside him, the Ghastly Horror rippled slightly, as if it were *swallowing,* greedily gulping down the lifeblood of the Dragon House. He realized that he was afraid too. Zarcon seemed to think this was such a great idea, but *he* wasn't willing to try it. What *would* happen when one started to cut the thing with the knife? It was dormant now, but surely that would wake it up...

He was level with its face. Suddenly, without detaching itself from its feeding, it twisted around toward him, and opened two glaring, red eyes.

Edward let out a yelp of surprise and fright and, before he was fully aware of what he was doing, he had grabbed onto the thing by its trumpet-mouth and was sawing through it furiously with the steak knife.

The Ghastly Horror shrieked *through* its widening wound, spread its enormous wings, and reached up at him with its claws, but just then he cut all the way through, and the Horror fell away from him, hit the floor, and *exploded* in a cloud of black smoke and dust.

Edward lost his balance and fell. Margaret fell, both of them landing in the billowing black mass. He heard Zarcon's motor roaring furiously, but paid no attention to that as, on hands and knees he groped blindly back into the side room where the librarian's crystal skull continued to complain about the mess.

"Young man, you need to pay more attention to your appearance before you come into this library. You are absolutely *filthy!*"

"Yeah, I know. Sorry."

Someone brushed against him. It was Margaret. She was filthy too, her face black as if she'd just crawled out of a coal chute.

Both of them just remained as they were for a while, coughing and gagging.

Behind them, Zarcon's motor roared.

Eventually Edward and Margaret both got up to see what was happening. They returned to the other room just in time to see Zarcon's extended hose vacuum up the last remains of the Ghastly Horror.

"Wow," said Edward. "I didn't know you could do that."

"This unit has its utility."

"But there's so much of it," Margaret said, indicting where the Horror had been. "Don't you have to change a bag or something?"

"No," said Zarcon. "The waste is dispersed into another dimension, where it will not trouble you. But before we proceed, we must improve our technique."

Edward tried to wipe the black dust off his face, but his hands were so dirty he could only smear it around. He coughed continuously. He had breathed in entirely too much of the stuff.

He coughed so hard he thought he would pass out, and couldn't say anything.

"Come to me, both of you," said Zarcon. They stood still while he vacuumed them both as best as could be managed, bidding them to crouch down so he could blow warm air on their hair and faces.

That felt a lot better. Edward could see that Margaret was still a complete mess, and was sure he was too. He realized that what he really, really wanted when all this was over was not a medal or to know the cosmic secrets of creation, but a nice, long, warm *bath*.

"We must find some way for you to protect yourselves," said Zarcon. "Ah, here—" He reached out and sucked a newspaper out of a cubbyhole, letting it stick at the mouth of his hose.

He switched his motor off for an instant and Edward took the paper from him. It was a very strange newspaper indeed. The pictures all seemed to be of insect-like creatures and the print was incomprehensible squiggles. Yet as he stared at it, the squiggles at the top resolved themselves into *The Betelgeuse Bugle*, and some of the text almost began to make sense.

"Don't read it," said Zarcon. "Take a page, wrap it around your head, and just make two holes for your eyes. It will have to do."

Edward and Margaret both did so, while from the next room the crystal skull whined, "No, no! Do not damage the periodicals! This is a *library!*"

"Sorry," Edward muttered, as he wrapped the newspaper over his head and stuffed the edges into the collar of his sweatshirt.

He saw that Margaret looked completely absurd like this, and he was sure that he did too. But there was no help for it.

He glanced up at the remaining Horrors. "Aren't they going to *notice* if we start chopping them down one by one?"

"In their feeding state, by daylight, they are very sluggish," said Zarcon. "Hurry. We must finish before it grows dark."

Edward was aware that, as often seemed to be happening in the course of his adventures, he had no idea what time it was, and it was even possible that time didn't pass at quite the same rate inside the house as it did in the outside world.

This gave him a certain sense of urgency. Therefore, grimly, he continued the work. Margaret seemed to sense the same thing, and no longer hesitated, as, one by one, they cleaned the library of Ghastly Horrors. The newspaper head-coverings helped. He found that if he closed his eyes and held his breath at the moment of each creature's dissolution it wasn't so bad.

Forty-six of them in all. It seemed to take hours, and there were several scary moments when the things halfway woke up, and hissed or howled or glared as they died, but Edward's stroke with the knife became sure and steady, like Doctor Van Helsing staking vampires.

When they were finally done, he and Margaret both slumped

down to the floor exhausted. He reached into another cubbyhole, took out another newspaper, and, despite wailing protests from the despairing librarian, used part of it in a further attempt at cleaning his hands and face. Margaret did the same. After a while, she remembered the groceries, went and got them, and the two of them made a cold supper while Zarcon's motor hummed contentedly, and little lights along the side of his vacuum-cleaner body, which Edward had not noticed before, blinked in sequence. Indeed, Zarcon never seemed to need to change a bag.

At last he made several whirring, buzzing, and beeping sounds which were perhaps the Zarconax equivalent of "Ahem!" and said, "We cannot tarry. We have no time. Look! It grows dark. Our enemies are far more dangerous in the dark."

Indeed it was. Shadows lengthened. Edward could see through the high windows of the library that the sun was going down.

"I think I know where we have to go next," he said.

Elsewhere in the house, the Ghastly Horrors began to stir and shriek. Edward could even hear their wings flapping, from all directions at once.

"I had hoped," said Zarcon, "to read through the books of magical lore with you and find some generally applicable solution to our difficulties, or at least review the opening chapter of *Ghastly Horrors and What To About Them—*"

"I think we know what to do about them," Edward said.

"I mean in terms of a more general solution, not a case-by-case instance."

"But like you said, there's no time."

"Indeed, there is not. Alas, there is not." Zarcon followed them, beeping and whirring, and Edward led them out of the library and onto the balcony overlooking the great windows, where the steering wheel now rolled gently from side to side. It hadn't been very long at all since Edward had been here with his father. He'd quite enjoyed that strange and wonderful time they'd had together, steering the house through the clouds and practicing gunnery.

"Oh my God, look at that!" Margaret suddenly shrieked when she saw the clouds outside the window now, racing past them, swirling over the twin observatory windows, sometimes blocking the view entirely, sometimes parting to reveal vast cloudscapes of green and blue and turquoise laced with crackling lightning. Above the cloud layer was a black sky, filled with stars. The Dragon House careened wildly, dipping into the clouds, lurching from side to side. The wheel rolled more and more, out of control.

"Where *are* we?" Margaret said. "Are we on Earth?"

"I don't know," said Edward. He saw three tiny moons in the sky, and so rather doubted they were on Earth. There was no time to worry about it. "I need you and Zarcon to go down below and operate the cannons."

"The *what?*"

He pointed to the stair that led down to the lower level. "Just do it. He'll know how. Dad showed me, but I have to stay up here."

She went, carrying Zarcon in her arms, since his short body and tiny wheels were not equipped to negotiate stairs.

Meanwhile Edward rolled up his jeans to his knees, and stood, legs apart, behind the "ship's wheel." He took hold of the wheel with both hands and concentrated on sharing the feelings of the House, of being *part* of the house. He sank into the floor, down to his knees, which put him in an awkward position since he was already too short for this wheel and sunken down like that he couldn't even see over the railing. But somehow the House knew what he needed and the floor swelled up like a bubble, raising him to a more comfortable level. He felt his fingers melting into the handles on the wheel, as if he were a part of it.

He felt what the Dragon House felt, as if the whole vast structure were, in some indefinable way, his own body. He was not comfortable. There was a great deal of pain and weariness, and he seemed to be covered with scabs, bitten constantly by mosquitos or, worse, leeches. His feet seemed stuck in something thick and cold and slowly congealing, with the added sensation that something was wriggling in it.

He had to concentrate very hard on what he was doing. His consciousness was split, as if he were the dragon itself, racing through the clouds, gazing out of the two observatory windows as if they were his own eyes, and at the same time standing on the balcony at the wheel trying to steer.

Now below he heard Margaret and Zarcon trying to figure out how to load the cannons.

He heard a cannonball roll down the chute and land with a clunk, like a bowling ball in a bowling alley. More than hearing it, he somehow *felt* it, almost as if he'd hiccupped deep within himself and burped up a cannonball.

He struggled with the wheel, trying to steady the Dragon House's flight, but the wheel only responded with difficulty. He imagined that it would be like this trying to steer a badly damaged ship, the holds half-filled with water, the vessel heavy and clumsy and slow to turn about.

Gradually he got it levelled out. Still the clouds raced below him. If there was any way to control speed he didn't know it. He could sense the mind of the Dragon itself, but distant and far away, and he could not speak to it. It wasn't fully awake or aware. It seemed to be streaking through the sky in blind panic, in the middle of a nightmare.

"Mags! How are you doing down there?"

"Almost got it."

Zarcon was saying something about "…stuff the wadding…no, in *there*…ramrod! Ramrod!…"

Something clicked like a cigarette lighter. Zarcon must have had some sort of attachment.

"I think we're ready!"

"Good! Make sure you don't stand behind the cannons when they go off! They really kick!"

"Are we shooting at something?"

"Uh," Edward said very softly, "I think so…"

He looked out the window again (and out of his own Dragon-eyes simultaneously) and saw *something* approaching from the far horizon, at first just a speck, but growing rapidly larger, dark, skimming across the cloud-tops. At first he thought it was a bird, but he misjudged its distance and size and took it for a jet fighter, then an even larger jet, as huge as a gigantic military cargo plane, then bigger yet, like an enormous black submarine with wings.

Flapping wings and a writhing, serpent-like neck.

Another dragon.

It loomed nearer and he could see details as it soared up out of the clouds, revealing its whole underside to him.

It was made of bones. The thing didn't look merely gaunt; it was without flesh, with a sagging black hide stretched over it like a tent over loosely-placed poles. This wasn't so much another dragon as the corpse of a dragon somehow animated.

He didn't have to wait long to see how. The thing swooped down, in front of him, nearer, and he could see that its back and wings were covered with millions of wriggling dark things like fleas or lice.

But not fleas or lice. He knew exactly what they were. This other dragon was completely covered (and no doubt filled) with Ghastly Horrors, like a dead animal you might see in a gutter, covered with ants.

"Gunnery!" Edward yelled.

"Ready!" Margaret yelled back.

The other dragon swooped up again, so close this time that the windows rattled with the wind of its passage.

"Fire!"

Nothing happened.

"Fire!" he yelled again.

"Sorry," Margaret replied. "The fuse went out!"

"Try again! Fire!"

More corpse-dragon roared past the windows like an express train. Its body began to taper into its tail.

The guns went off, first one, then the other three. Edward saw the impacts, little bursts of flame on the body of the corpse-dragon, like random hits on the surface of the Death Star in *Star Wars* and about as effectual.

"Fire!"

"Give us time to reload first!"

"Fire!"

The enemy swooped down again, then turned directly toward Edward, its eyes blazing, its mouth open and streaming smoke.

"Fire!"

The enemy drifted off to the left. No, it was the Dragon House. Edward struggled to turn the wheel with all his might, but the "vessel" was indeed "sluggish at the helm," turning slowly, heavily, painfully as Edward strained every muscle.

The enemy was almost in the center of his view again when all four guns went off almost simultaneously. Somewhere, deep within himself, he felt the recoil. He saw that two shots missed but the other two actually managed to smash the bottom half of the enemy's right eye. Black and red fragments flew, gleaming as they tumbled through space. Smoke poured out of the wound.

But the enemy kept coming. It opened its mouth wider, until he could see its teeth, like the sharp ridgeline of a mountain. Then from somewhere within that terrible maw, the enemy's own gunnery opened fire, dozens of shots at once, all of them finding their mark, crashing into the house. He felt as if he had been slugged in the gut, hard, and he reeled back, struggling to breathe, desperately clinging to the wheel.

"Fire!" he gasped. "Fire! Fire!"

One more shot issued from his own guns, to no effect. The observatory windows exploded inward, the rush of the blast knocking Edward away from the wheel entirely, uprooting him from the floor, and sending him skidding in a shower of glass, until he slammed against a wall and sat there, limply, only half-conscious, nearly blinded as the air filled with black dust and swirling green fumes that smelled like floor cleaner and hurt his lungs as if he were trying to inhale knives. Thousands of Ghastly Horrors poured in through the ruined windows and filled the air with the thunder of their wings.

He heard his sister screaming and Zarcon's motor whirring furiously, but then they were gone.

He was somehow still in touch with the Dragon House, enough to share its senses. It seemed that something stifling and foul, like a bag full of industrial waste had dropped over his head.

The enemy dragon, the corpse-dragon, had swallowed them all.

For a while he lay in darkness, unable to see, straining desperately to breathe, tears streaming from his eyes.

Then he could see, a little, and a familiar person in a black uniform stood over him.

"Hello, Edward," she said. "Remember me? You have caused entirely enough trouble for us, but I can assure you that your resistance is at an end."

He tried to turn and crawl away, but he couldn't control his limbs. He managed to roll on one side, when something grabbed him by the hair with rough claws and, mimicking the previous speaker, said in a voice that was not human at all, "Hello, Edward, remember me?"

And a Ghastly Horror, with its teeth spread wide, lowered its black trumpet-shaped mouth over his face, and he knew nothing more.

Chapter Ten
Mrs. Morgentod Again

Edward awoke slowly, groggily, as if from a nightmare that didn't want to let him go. He was sitting in a cramped schoolroom desk-and-chair, and feeling terribly uncomfortable, itchy all over, with what felt like powdered glass grinding into his skin where he sat, and against his back, and under his arms.

His vision cleared, and he indeed seemed to be in a schoolroom. At least there was a blackboard in front of him and a teacher's desk.

The air was thick with swirling dust. He sneezed and coughed.

"Edward...?"

He turned to his right, and saw Margaret also seated at a desk-and-chair a little in front of his, looking very dirty, very bedraggled, and clad in an orange jumpsuit like the one he'd been given at the "police station," only what was written on the back left much less to the imagination. It said merely: SLAVE.

He was wearing such a suit too, and the inside of it was filthy and gritty. He didn't doubt that his also said SLAVE on the back.

"I'm okay," he whispered back, although he did not feel okay at all. But he wanted to reassure Margaret and he couldn't think of anything else to say.

Whap!!

A wooden pointer slammed down on the desktop in front of him. He looked up suddenly.

"Good *morning*, children!"

He looked up and saw standing in front of him a very familiar figure, all in black but for the silver skulls on her lapels. Above her, Ghastly Horrors sagged from the walls and ceiling, like boils from diseased skin.

The woman paced back and forth between Edward's desk and Margaret's, tapping her palm with her pointer. Unlike a typical teacher's pointer this one did not have a rubber tip. The end of it looked to

THE DRAGON HOUSE | 103

be capped with metal.

"I am Mrs. Morgentod. Edward and I have met before. You, Margaret, I now have the pleasure of meeting for the first time."

Margaret glared at her.

Whap!! The pointer slammed down on Margaret's desk, quick enough to catch the back of her hand. Margaret yelped.

"You haven't been very polite, but no matter. Henceforth I am your mother, father, family, master, and owner. I demand the utmost respect and obedience."

"You and what army?" Margaret muttered under her breath.

Whap!! This time the pointer hit her on the side of the face. Edward could see that it left a bloody welt on her cheek.

Mrs. Morgentod wrote the word EVIL on the blackboard with a piece of chalk.

"The organization we all serve—you two included, you most especially Edward—is commonly known as FOD, which some ignorant people think it amusing to pronounce as if it rhymed with "odd." It stands quite simply for Forces of Darkness. You are no doubt making moral judgments even as you sit there. You think that we are EVIL, that we are unabashedly the Bad Guys, and I suppose, in a sense you are correct. *We* do not hesitate. *We* do not go into self-pitying paroxysms of doubt about 'Did I do the right thing?' and 'Is this honorable?' and 'What would my mommy want me to do?'"

As Mrs. Morgentod spoke, she marched back and forth, glaring at Margaret, then at Edward, then at Margaret again. She seemed quite full of herself, impressed to hear herself talk.

"*We* are the party of the strong," she continued. "We *take* what we want and don't ask anyone's permission. Our *strength* is the only justification we need."

"Sounds like fascism to me," Margaret whispered, furious.

Again, quick as a striking snake, the pointer swung at Margaret, who ducked this time. The metal-tipped point swished through the air over her head. Margaret stuck out her tongue in contempt, but only for an instant, as Mrs. Morgentod landed blows on the back of her head and on her shoulders.

"Stop that!" Edward screamed. He tried to get up, and only then discovered that he was chained by his ankles to the legs of his desk and the desk itself was bolted to the floor. Margaret, too, was chained to her desk by her ankles, which was why she hadn't been able to get away. Her shoes were gone. She was as barefoot as he was.

Mrs. Morgentod went on beating her, *whap! whap! whap!* as if she were beating a rug.

"Stop that!"

Suddenly she turned toward Edward and marched, like a robot, with perfect military precision.

"You do not *command* me, Edward. *Not even you.* You may beg, plead, grovel, but *never* command!"

Edward sat back down in his chair. He looked fearfully over at Margaret, who was lying head-down, possibly unconscious.

"Well," said Mrs. Morgentod, flipping her pointer under her arm as if it were a riding crop, "now that that's settled, I may resume today's lesson. While there may be no right and wrong in the universe, what we of the FOD do is for the *best* because we represent *order* and *order* is for the *best*. Therefore you should respect the actual *benevolence* of our mission."

"Yeah, and Attila the Hun meant well," Margaret mumbled blearily.

Mrs. Morgentod turned quickly toward Margaret again, just as Edward made another attempt to stand yanking hard against the metal cuffs that held his bare ankles.

"Stop hitting her—!"

Just as suddenly Mrs. Morgentod whirled around and struck Edward full across the face with her pointer. He flopped back into his seat in shock as she shouted, "Try that again and you will find yourself *nailed* in your place—but not before I've done the same thing to your sister."

Mrs. Morgentod, furious, was truly hideous to look upon. Edward lowered his head. He realized that his nose was bleeding. He sputtered red droplets onto the grimy desktop.

The pointer prodded him under the chin and raised his head.

"Edward, *you* are of some use to us because of your *special* relationship to the Dragon House. You are like a customized component in the guidance system. Not essential. You can be replaced, but it is *convenient* for us to keep you alive and *use* you. Your sister, however, is just an ordinary girl, and of no use to us whatsoever, except as a means of influencing you. Which means, in words of one syllable, if you are bad, she gets hit *first*. So *stay put*. Do what you are told and only what you are told."

"*I want to know what happened to my Mom and Dad!*" Edward screamed. "I'm not doing anything until you tell me!"

The pointer swung again. Edward ducked and it actually swept through the top of his hair. Then Mrs. Morgentod seemed to remember her initial threat, went back to beating on Margaret for a while, until dust rose from Margaret's jumpsuit in clouds.

Edward could only put his head down on his desk, cover his ears and sob, "Stop it! Stop it!" He pulled desperately, trying to slide his feet out through the cuffs, but to no avail.

Margaret said nothing. She lay still.

Then the pointer poked Edward in the face.

"Sit up."

He sat up.

"You still haven't figured it out yet, have you Edward? I shall try again, in very simple language. You have no choices. You don't get to bargain. You have nothing with which to negotiate. You cannot make demands."

"What if I have to go to the bathroom?" Edward asked softly, with just a trace of defiance left in his voice.

"That is a privilege to be earned. If you do not earn it, I guess you will be just a dirtier and smellier little boy than before."

Unthinkingly, Edward fingered the golden dragon-scale he still wore around his neck. Despite everything, the enemy had not been able to remove it.

Mrs. Morgentod poked him one more time with the pointer.

"And you mustn't think, Edward, that…object…is going to do you any good. All we have to do is *cut your head off*, then turn your corpse upside down, and your little trinket will drop away all by itself. So sit still, shut up, and obey. *Have I made myself clear?*"

"Yes, Ma'am."

"Better."

Just then someone knocked at the doorway and a man in a uniform similar to hers came in, saluted, and presented her with a clipboard.

"I see," she said to him. "Unaccounted for?"

The man mumbled something Edward couldn't make out.

"Very well," said Mrs. Morgentod. "I will see to it personally. But I assure you, heads are going to roll for this."

The man saluted again, expressionless, turned, and marched out of the room.

Mrs. Morgentod turned back to Edward and Margaret.

"I am called away on a minor matter," she said. "I leave you to think about what you have learned today, but first, I have something to show you."

She reached down below her desk and lifted up a large cardboard box, which she dumped out onto the desktop. Metal clanged and rattled, Pieces bounced to the floor and rolled in every direction, but enough remained on the desktop for Edward to recognize, with a sinking, sickening feeling of helplessness, the smashed remains of a vacuum cleaner body and the head of Zarcon of Zarconax. No lights were blinking. His head, though not smashed, looked like a piece of junk.

"This is how much help you can expect from your various friends and family members," said Mrs. Morgentod. "Don't get your hopes up."

With that, she flipped her pointer under her arm, turned and marched out of the room.

Only when her footsteps had faded down the corridor outside did Edward dare whisper, "Mags?" He was sniffling, a combination of tears and his bloody nose.

Silence.

"Mags?"

His sister groaned, then said, "I'm okay." She did not raise her head.

"You don't sound okay."

"Got a few lumps, I guess."

"I'm not going to stay here," he said. "I'd rather die."

"Me too."

"Do you think we'll have to?" Edward realized that he actually had little idea of what he was talking about it. He just talked to sound brave, to keep his own spirits up.

"Very probably."

"There has to be another way," said Edward.

"Like what?"

THE DRAGON HOUSE | 107

"I don't know. But the first one of us to get away should grab Zarcon's head. I don't think the rest of him matters. Take it to Doctor Basileus or to Dad or someone. They'll know what to do."

"And where are they?"

"No idea," said Edward. "I have no ideas about anything." He put his head down on the desktop again. He wished he could sleep, to make all this go away even temporarily, but he couldn't. He felt very weak, exhausted, and he hurt all over, but the situation just refused to end.

Margaret lowered her head to her desk and lay still, her hands hanging limply over either side.

"Mags?"

She didn't reply. He struggled again. He rattled his chains. But there was no way he could get to her. She'd been hit on the head several times. What if she had a concussion? It would be bad for her to go to sleep.

She could *die* like that.

And there was nothing he could do. Nothing.

He realized that this was the lowest, darkest point of his life. He was truly afraid now, truly helpless, entirely ready to give in utterly to despair, just barely clinging to the idea that somehow, for some reason he couldn't quite formulate, he shouldn't.

The only thing he could bring to mind as even the slightest excuse for hope was something his father had once said. His father could be goofy at times, and maybe, Edward had begun to suspect, quite incompetent, but every once in a while he had said something genuinely wise, such as: *Well, when you're in trouble, you can just stick your finger up your nose, moan, "Oh woe is me, I can't cope," then roll over and die with your legs in the air like a bug—or not.*

Edward definitely preferred the *or not* option. He just didn't know how to get to it.

He kept on pulling with his feet, trying to break out of the ankle cuffs until he realized how much that actually hurt. He leaned over, looked down, and saw that he'd cut himself rather badly in the struggle. Both of his feet were covered with blood. It felt sticky between his toes.

His hands were bloody too, mostly from where he'd tried to wipe his nose. His actual nosebleed had stopped.

But there was a lot of blood everywhere, on his face, on the desktop…and this was how the idea came to him, not so much out of rational deductive thought, but as if, half-consciously the pieces drifted together. Blood and flesh. Touching. Feet and hands. He had, he had been told, a kind of *affinity* for the Dragon House that no one else seemed to share. *He* could push his hands, or his face, or his entire body right through the walls or floor and the house *accepted* him. *He* could swim through that strange space between the walls like some sort of tiny but not unwelcome creature inside the Dragon's own bloodstream, almost as if he were actually a *part* of the Dragon. He could reach the Dragon's heart and brain. *He* could converse with the Dragon.

All this was possible through some strange communion of flesh— and blood.

He could call on the Dragon, if only he could somehow *touch* it.

But he wasn't even sure where he was. *His* dragon had been swallowed, at least in part, by the other, by the dead thing. He could envision the two of them tumbling through space, the mouth of the dead thing having closed over the neck and head of his own dragon, the way one snake swallows another, slowly engulfing and digesting it even while part of the body still hangs out of the predator's mouth, loose and limp.

Somehow, in ways he did not understand, a dragon could also be a house. It could make rooms come into existence.

So, was this "schoolroom" inside *his* dragon or the other?

Or, as one swallowed the other, did they merge together?

Did it really matter?

Was *his* dragon, *the* Dragon of the Dragon House, still alive? Could he still get a message out to it?

He scraped the dust away from the floor with one big toe. He pressed his foot down and spread out his toes.

Nothing. No contact.

But this floor was covered with dirty, cracked linoleum tiles that curled upward at the edges. Under that? Far under that…?

If only he could melt, flow down like water.

He knew he couldn't; but he knew now what he had to do.

At least it looked like a good idea at the moment, and he couldn't think beyond the moment.

He judged his left ankle to be the messier and bloodier of the two. Therefore, gritting his teeth, he pulled *hard* with his left leg, also yanking on his leg with both of his hands. He couldn't allow himself to stop, no matter how much it hurt, and it hurt quite a bit. In fact the pain drove him into a frenzy of effort. Tears streamed down his face and he was gasping for breath, and he'd come very close to pulling his left foot out of the metal cuff.

But that wasn't the point. The point was that his blood now flowed freely, onto the floor, between the cracks, under the linoleum tiles, down, down, until someone or something could feel or sense in some unimaginable way that he was there. If the Dragon was still alive, it would find him, by the scent and touch and possibly the taste of his blood; by that fellowship, sameness, the mysterious *affinity* they two shared.

It was a good theory anyway. He pulled so hard that he started to faint. The room darkened and began to shift, as if he were in an elevator that dropped with one sickening lurch after another, but never seemed to hit anything.

He tried to reach over with his right foot to help smear the blood from his left, but there wasn't enough chain on the cuff, and he couldn't reach.

This was just going to have to work. Maybe it would have been quicker if Mrs. Morgentod *had* nailed his foot to the floor. That would have gotten the blood further down into the living wood of the Dragon House, if there still *was* any living wood, if the Ghastly Horrors (which were starting to stir and stretch their wings, as the room darkened) hadn't sucked all the life out of it.

He yanked again and he actually did get his left foot loose, though he was still bleeding badly. Now he could smear his own blood around quite freely, like fingerpaint, only with his toes, over the cracks and the holes in the floor.

He tried to project his thoughts, to think like a radio and just broadcast, *Help me help me help me come and get me get me...*

And then the most astonishing thing happened. The blackboard fell off the wall with a loud crash and smashed against Mrs. Morgentod's desk.

Someone dressed all in white, who looked a little like a hospital nurse, but for her tall, pointed cap, was standing there as chalk dust settled.

Edward refused to believe his eyes. He was sure he'd passed out and was dreaming, and the horrible conclusion would be that somehow the figure in white was going to tell him that: *No, this rescue is the dream. You're still stuck chained to that desk and no one is coming to save you. You have to wake up now, Dear—*

Instead, he said, *"Mom?"*

"Edward! Are you hurt?"

"A little, I guess—"

She hurried over to him and he saw that she was indeed dressed in flowing white, with a pointed white hat—he hadn't hallucinated any of it. Furthermore, she wore a name badge like a hospital employee might wear, with her name and a little picture and the words GOOD WITCHES UNION, LOCAL 101.

She took him by the chin and gave him a critical look, as if checking to see if his nose was broken (it wasn't) or if his skull was bashed in (fortunately not).

Then she opened her robe a little. He saw she was wearing a utility belt such as an electrician might use to hold his tools while climbing a telephone pole. She selected a wand.

"This will hurt a little," she said, but before he could react she reached down and touched the cuff on his right ankle with the wand.

The metal became so cold it burned.

She put the wand away and got out an ordinary household hammer, then tapped firmly on the cuff a couple times. The cuff shattered.

Edward lurched up. She had to catch him to help him stand. They stood in an awkward embrace, her name-badge inches away from his face.

"Mom, I didn't know you—"

"Neither did your father, Edward. He probably thought I was going to book clubs or playing bingo. He thinks I'm just a housewife. Sometimes it's useful for people to underestimate you."

Then another thought crossed his mind and he broke away.

"Mags!"

He lurched toward his sister but his legs folded under him and he fell to his hands and knees. He started crawling furiously. She was only about six or eight feet away, but it seemed an impossible distance.

His mother hauled him up and sat him on the teacher's desk.

"It's all right, Edward. It's all right!"

"Mom, she's hurt—"

Mom got out the wand and the hammer, and set Margaret free. She had to help her to her feet, and Edward saw that Margaret was a total mess, covered with dust, with blood on her face from more than one scalp wound, but she stood steadily and pushed her matted hair out of her eyes.

"I'll be fine," she said. "Thanks, Edward. Thanks, Mom."

Just then there were sharp, hard footsteps in the corridor outside.

Edward felt a stab of terror. He knew that gait.

And he knew the voice that said, "No one is going to get away with anything! Defiance will not be tolerated!"

Margaret glared, then muttered, "You know, I'd really love to shove that pointer where she doesn't want it."

Mom moved into action. She lifted Edward to his feet, then got out her wand.

"No. You two have to get out of here, now. Margaret, help your brother."

Margaret put her arm around Edward and steadied him. "Can you stand?" she asked him.

"Yeah."

"Can you run?"

"If I have to."

The footsteps and threatening voice drew nearer. "No defiance! No resistance! No inefficiency!"

There were other footsteps too, some of them softer and shuffling.

"I think you're going to have to," said Mom. "Go!"

"Where?"

"There. That way." She pointed to a large, heavy door, arched at the top like a church door. Edward hadn't noticed it before because it had been behind him when he was chained to the desk.

Margaret hauled Edward over to the door. Both of them grabbed the iron ring and pulled with all their might to get the door open. Slowly it swung into the room.

Then Edward let go. "Wait! Wait!"

"Wait for what?"

He lurched painfully over to the desk, scooped up Zarcon of Zarconax's head and hurried back to rejoin Margaret.

Then Mrs. Morgentod stood in the other doorway, confronting Mrs. Longstretch of Good Witches Local 101.

"You!"

"Yeah, me," said Mom in a tone more suitable for a western gunfighter. "*Unaccounted for.* What are you going to do about it?"

Mrs. Morgentod *shrieked*, making a sound that could never have come from a purely human throat, like a whole chorus of Ghastly Horrors sounding off all at once. The shock of it hit Edward and Margaret like a wind, and almost blew them off their feet. It *did* blow the door shut again.

Now Mrs. Morgentod was joined by dozens of guards, variously armed with swords, pikes, and submachineguns. Some of them had human heads and faces, some not.

Facing them all was only one white witch with her wand.

"Mom! Mom!" Edward cried out.

"Go! Find Miss Emily! I'll take care of them! Go!"

It was quite to their advantage that Margaret was such a big girl, that she was considerably stronger than Edward, particularly when she was right at the edge of panic.

She managed to get the door open just enough. She shoved Edward through and followed, as the room filled with explosions and the flash of lightning, and a roaring wind slammed the door closed again behind them.

Chapter Eleven
Miss Emily Again

It was like a funhouse that wasn't fun. They made their way in absolute darkness along a corridor that swayed and twisted and sagged like a rope bridge. Sometimes the floor rippled. Once it threw both of them over to the right and backwards, so that they landed in a heap, Margaret on top of Edward, Edward desperately groping around for Zarcon's head, which he'd dropped as he tumbled.

It took the both of them several minutes, crawling around on the heaving floor, to find the head. Edward took it. Then he strained to get to his feet and couldn't quite do it. His left ankle hurt terribly. He didn't know if he was still bleeding, but it still felt sticky between his toes. He caught hold of Margaret and she hauled him up.

"Are you going to make it?" she whispered.

"I can't stay here."

That seemed to settle things. They proceeded, slowly. Margaret seemed to have recovered better than Edward had. More than once she paused for him to catch up, and they groped about and found one another in the dark. Then it occurred to him to hold his sister's hand, and she took hold of him without a word, gently pulling him along.

All the while the head of Zarcon of Zarconax in his other hand was just a cold, dead thing, like the head of a parking meter.

The "floor" was made of—Edward wasn't sure what. It felt like crumbling leather beneath his bare feet. It was as if they were walking on an enormous, decaying trampoline, which heaved and shifted with their weight yet threatened to split and give way at any moment.

"Look," said Margaret, tugging him toward her. "Up there."

For a minute he thought it was a trick of his eyes, like the drifting blobs you can sometimes see behind your eyelids if you close your eyes tightly. But then he realized that it was more steady than that: a faint spot of light, or perhaps a slightly shifting rectangle, like the opening of a tent flapping in a breeze, leading from absolute blackness into a gray gloom that was, by comparison, a tremendous relief, or would be, if only they could get to it.

The opening was far ahead of them, and *up* a ways.

Edward let Margaret lead him, almost drag him as the floor sloped upward toward that light. Now the going was a little easier. The floor seemed a little more solid, almost like wood, if soft and splintery on the surface, like the surface of a rotten log. At least it had stopped heaving. It even began to shape itself, gradually, into something almost like stairs, a series of gradual rises and bumps. The walls around them were likewise solid now, and Margaret was able to reach out with her free hand occasionally and steady herself.

The opening grew larger.

"Almost there," she whispered.

That was when she fell through the floor.

With a scream she dropped, but retained her hold on Edward's hand, and so dragged him down onto his knees. Fortunately she hadn't fallen all the way through, but had been caught under the armpits.

"Edward! Help me!"

He pulled as hard as he could with the one arm, but it wasn't enough. She was struggling, twisting.

"It's open below me," she said. "I don't know how far down. Use both hands!"

But how could he use both hands if he had to hang on to Zarcon's head? Somehow he knew that it would be an unimaginable catastrophe if they lost Zarcon, either by letting him roll back down the way they'd come in the dark or, worse yet, by letting him drop down the same hole Margaret had fallen into, either after he got her out or she fell all the way in.

She struggled more, trying to grab on with her free hand.

"It's too loose! It's crumbling!"

Edward had to pause for just a second to consider, but only a second. If he'd had a free hand, he could have unzipped the front of his jumpsuit, stuffed Zarcon inside, zipped it up again, and gone on to rescue Margaret, however awkward that might have been.

But he didn't have a free hand. The only solution, however ridiculous it would have looked if there had been enough light for either one of them to have seen that much, was to put the stub of Zarcon's neck in his mouth—he could just barely do it—and clamping tight with his teeth and jaws, while bracing his feet against the floor and grabbing hold of Margaret's wrist with both hands.

"Edward! I think there's something down here with me! Something touched my foot!"

"Mmmmfff!" was all he could reply. He pulled with all his strength. Somehow it was enough. She heaved herself up, wriggled, and caught hold of a more solid section of flooring. She let go of him and began to crawl. He crawled after her, first taking Zarcon back into his right hand. He spat. His mouth tasted of machine oil and dust. He was able to make a sound like "Bleh!" then spit some more.

Now the upward slope of the floor was too steep for them to stand, so they hand to continue on all fours. Edward paused for just a second to unzip the front of his jumpsuit, stuff Zarcon inside, and zip up. The metal was cold against his chest.

As they climbed toward the light, he was less and less sure they were going to make it. More than once his hand or his foot or his knee broke through the floor, into the emptiness below. He didn't know how far down it was. He didn't care to find out. But if the whole floor gave way at once, they *would* find out. It might be the last thing they'd ever learn.

"Spread out," he said to Margaret.

"What?"

"We can't stay too close together. It'll make the floor break."

She got the idea. He stayed still for a moment while she moved on ahead of him, and gingerly they both climbed, extending their hands and feet out to spread their weight. Crumbling bits of rotten flooring rained down over him. He had to shake his head to keep them out of his face. He heard the debris rattling down into the darkness behind him.

Then she was at the top. She was standing in the doorway. She reached down to give him a hand. He caught hold of her hand. She started to pull him up.

Then *something* grabbed him by both ankles.

Now it was his turn to let out a scream, and she grabbed him by the wrist with both her hands and heaved, while he caught hold of her wrist with his free hand. But whatever had him was heavy and strong, and was pulling him back into the darkness.

He kicked as hard as he could with his right foot, got partly clear, and kicked again. It felt as if he'd kicked something hard and round and smooth, like a bowling ball, only slimy. Still Margaret and whatever it was played tug-of-war with Edward, pulling so hard it felt like his arms and legs would be ripped out of their sockets.

He struggled, twisting, and tried to kick again. No good.

But the enemy, whatever it was, shifted its grip slightly, and this allowed Margaret to pull him further out into the light.

Now he could *see* what held him, or at least part if it.

Clasping him by the ankles were two pale hands, almost human in their shape, but the fingers were much too long.

And there were two *more* such hands, one on either side, bracing against the sides of the passage.

Then he saw the face, likewise almost human, but at the same time flat, blank, almost featureless but for two over-large, watery eyes and a small oval mouth lined with needle-like teeth.

The body, such as he could make it out, was not human at all, more insectoid, with an indeterminate number of limbs, and the appearance overall rather like a louse or mite of some sort seen under a microscope.

Only there was no microscope. This one bigger than he was.

And as he watched, another such face appeared out of the darkness, its watery eyes squinting at even the pale gray light from behind Margaret.

This was joined by another, and another.

Edward let go of Margaret's wrist with his left hand. The result was to make Margaret partially lose her grip and he almost slid down into the darkness again, but in the intervening seconds he unzipped the front of his jumpsuit, grabbed hold of Zarcon's metal neck, and, swinging Zarcon's head like a club, hit the round, pale face right between its enormous eyes. He hit it once, then again, then a third time, with all his strength, until he felt something crunch. The monster let out a hiss and a high-pitched shriek, released its grip, and tumbled down into the tunnel, bowling over its fellows, even as Margaret tumbled over backwards and hauled Edward out with her.

They landed in a heap, untangled themselves and got up. Edward stood, hefting Zarcon's head. There were chittering and squealing sounds from within the passageway but nothing emerged.

"Are you all right?" Margaret asked.

"Yeah. Thanks."

"Good thing you had…him with you." She indicated the metal head.

"Sorry, Zarcon," Edward said to the head. "I had to do it. I hope I didn't break anything."

"On…on…on…the contrary," replied Zarcon. "That is exactly what I needed. A sound jolt to get me going…"

Edward almost dropped the head in surprise, but didn't. He turned it until it was facing him, and he saw that while one of the eyes was smashed, the other flickered dimly.

"Zarcon! Are you all right?"

"I have been better, I must admit, but this is no time for pleasantries and social chit-chat, Edward. You and your sister must keep moving. Those creatures are afraid of the light, but when it gets dark, they will swarm by the hundreds."

"Where should we go?"

"Turn around. Look."

Edward and Margaret both turned. He realized they were in the room of the enormous carousel, where he had been before, only now the place was dim and so thick with dust and cobwebs that the effect was as if all the wooden creatures were draped in cloth like old furniture.

Yet the carousel figures were moving slowly. Somewhere beneath the floor, a mechanism ground uncertainly.

"Get on. Mount," said Zarcon.

"But, shouldn't we just run?"

"No, get on."

They got on, gagging at the clouds of dust stirred up as they did. When Edward could see even a little bit again, the carousel seemed to be moving somewhat faster, but still grinding haltingly around in a circle.

"Turn, turn," said Zarcon of Zarconax, who was still held in Edward's hand. "It turns, to show you the way."

The carousel made a complete circuit. Edward looked fearfully toward the opening from which they had emerged, but the opening wasn't there anymore. The carousel turned again and there was quite a different opening, with pillars on either side of it like the doorway to a temple.

"No, not that one," said Zarcon.

After carousel's third rotation, and there was no opening at all. The room was getting darker.

Then another, very ordinary wooden door drifted into view, slightly ajar.

"There! Dismount!"

They got down and stepped off the edge of the turning carousel, onto a little lip of stationary floor.

Margaret opened the door and they all went through.

On the other side was an ordinary wooden stairway. When Edward stepped on this with his bare feet he could feel the flesh of the Dragon House, cold, its consciousness very far away, but still definitely alive.

It was a very good sign.

He and Margaret hurried up the steps and emerged into a familiar, antique bedroom, and a familiar friendly voice said, "Well hello dearies. Aren't you two a mess?"

Margaret hesitated, but Edward pushed past her.

"Hello Miss Emily. Mom said to find you. I guess we did."

It was indeed Miss Emily, dressed in an old-fashioned dress with lots of lace, her hair up in a bun, classic "granny glasses" on her face. Again, she almost seemed like something out of a good dream, from which Edward was afraid he would suddenly awaken.

Margaret said, dubiously, "Do you two know each other?"

"Well, yes," said Edward. "She gave me the slippers. Remember?"

Margaret had that "I think I will just go mad again" look, but only for a moment. She was getting used to things, Edward realized. He knew he could rely on her.

"Greetings...Emily Armitage, former mistress of the Dragon House," said Zarcon of Zarconax.

"Oh, I see you've brought friend of mine," said Miss Emily.

"We are of long-time acquaintance," Zarcon explained.

"I think he needs some fixing," said Margaret.

"I think you all do," said Miss Emily, wincing sympathetically as he noticed how badly Edward was limping. "Come here," she said to him, directing him to sit on the bed. "Let me have a look."

She examined Edward's ankles, particularly the left, which was a ghastly, oozing mess of dirt and blood.

"Oh, that's nasty. I bet it hurts."

"It does," said Edward.

"I am afraid this will sting a bit." She took up what might well have been the very same bottle of alcohol and the same towel Margaret had used on Edward a while ago in this very room (or was it the same room, or a mirror of it?) and started to swab.

It hurt quite a bit, but Edward was brave, and hardly squirmed at all.

"You ought to have that looked at when you can," she said, "by a real doctor. It might get infected."

"Okay," said Edward between gasps. "I will."

"I can't do much more for you now, I'm afraid. You'll have to hurry."

"Hurry?"

Miss Emily didn't answer, but was tending to Margaret, who had the equivalent of burns on her ankles, where her own chains had been frozen and broken off.

Edward let go of Zarcon's head and let him roll onto the bed.

"The enemy is in close pursuit," said Zarcon. "We cannot pause. We cannot rest. The house has been taken over. We are in enemy territory now."

"What happened to Mom?" Edward asked.

"She held them back for a time, creating a useful diversion. It was excellently done."

Now Miss Emily spoke up. "Edward, don't worry about your mother. She is a person of many surprises."

"Yeah, I know."

"She will be able to take care of herself and very likely create even more useful diversions. But Zarcon is right, dear. You must get on with your mission. You can't rest until you see this through to the end."

"My mission? See what through?"

She seemed to change the subject. "And now I imagine you two children would just love to get out of those horrible, itchy suits!"

She opened a drawer and tossed Margaret some kind of old-fashioned gown or dress in a checkerboard pattern. "My old gingham," she said, and tossed it to Margaret who gladly changed into it.

"And Edward, you must wear only this."

She was holding what looked like little more than a belt, made of what might have been a very thin leather or snakeskin.

"It is a piece of the hide of the King Dragon, the master dragon and father of all dragons, whose scale you wear around your neck" she explained. "He molts periodically, like any lizard. Fragments go drifting around the universe. We try to gather them up when we can. They really come in quite handy sometimes."

"But...I'll look like Tarzan."

Nevertheless, he did as she instructed, and got out of his jumpsuit with great relief. It took a moment to figure out how to get the dragon skin to stay in place. It was an art, like tying a tie. He realized he'd never actually seen Tarzan getting dressed in a movie. After a couple of tries, he wrapped the dragon skin around himself the way it was supposed to go, tied it around his waist with the knot in the back, then folded the long flap under and over and arranged it in the front like an apron.

He noticed then that there was a large mirror on the nightstand. From what he could see of himself he didn't look like Tarzan at all, but like a scrawny cartoon character who had just suffered a dynamite explosion, covered head to foot with soot and grime, his eyes wide, white circles, his hair frazzled out every which way.

The dragon scale that he wore below his chin was glowing.

Now Miss Emily placed her hands on both of Edward's shoulders and steadied him, and looked straight into his eyes and said, "Edward, you must realize that it is time for you to become a hero. Nothing less will do. I am sorry—everyone is sorry—that this is necessary now, that you did not have years to prepare and train and learn and grow. But things have not worked out according to plan."

"Uh-huh. I know that."

"You also know perfectly well why you must wear only the skin of the King Dragon. It is because of where you must go and what you must do. You must swim through the Dragon's blood to reach the Dragon's heart. You have to be able to move freely, without any hindrance, in the place of which you are a part. Everything, and I mean *everything*, including the lives of your family, your friends, the very existence of this planet, depends on your success. Now I would like to help you more than I can. If I could, I'd give you a suit of unbreakable armor and a portable cannon, but I can't. I can offer you this, though, which will have to do."

Somewhat ceremoniously, she turned, took something out of another drawer, unwrapped the cloth from around it, and presented him with what could only be described as a very large dagger or a short sword. It was as long as his forearm. The handle and grip seemed to be of hardened leather, scaled, possibly more dragon-hide. The scabbard was made of the same material. He slid the blade out and saw that it gleamed a pale white. It looked more like ivory than metal. The weapon felt very light in his hand.

"A fragment of the tooth of the King Dragon," Miss Emily said. "He sheds those too, like a shark does. Use it well, Edward."

"Uh, okay..." He didn't know what else to say. He knew that it was just about time for him to leave, to begin his quest or battle or whatever it was. He thought back to his previous notion about silly movies, sending hundred-pound boys up against five-hundred pound monsters and the likely result of red, lumpy smears across the landscape. But he knew he *had* to go. A major part of being a hero is realizing that you have to do what needs to be done *when* it needs to be done, not at your convenience.

Margaret stared at him, the look on her face a strange mixture of admiration and much more that he couldn't sort out. She looked like she might be about to cry.

"I'll be all right, Mags. I'll see you in a little while."

"Okay," she said.

Then he turned back to Miss Emily and said, "One more thing. Can I have something to drink first?" He would have gone on to explain that they'd been fighting and running for hours, breathing dust and soot and cobwebs and worse, and his throat was horribly dry and his tongue felt like sandpaper, but Miss Emily merely said, "Why of course, dearie," and pulled out from under her bed a very modern, plastic cooler, from which she got out two bottles of spring water. One she gave to Edward and the other she tossed to Margaret.

Edward drank long and deep until his head hurt from the sudden cold. There was a little left over. He cupped some of it in his hand and tried to wash the worst of the grime off himself, but only succeeded in smearing it around. Another thing he was coming to realize is that a real, working hero doesn't have much time to look after his appearance.

He turned to Miss Emily.

"I guess I'm ready now."

"Bye, bye, dearie."

"Bye."

He slid the dragon-tooth knife and scabbard into the side of his loincloth, just as Tarzan would do. Then he crouched down on the floor. The wood began to ripple. He let his feet sink in a little bit. After a moment he leaned forward and dove through the floor, sliding into darkness smoothly, without meeting the slightest resistance.

Chapter Twelve
In the Bloodstream

No more than two weeks previously, Edward realized, he'd been a normal kid dressed in shorts, a t-shirt, and sneakers, riding a skateboard along a Northeast Philadelphia street on his way to return a library book.

Things can change very fast. He doubted anything in his life would ever be "normal" again. That skateboard ride seemed like a strange dream he could only half-remember.

Now, nearly naked, he swam in almost complete darkness through what he could only, in some abstract way, describe to himself as the *bloodstream* of the living house. But the sensation wasn't nearly as pleasant as it was the first time he'd taken a dive through his bedroom floor. Now the house was very sick, perhaps dying. It had been swallowed by another dragon, and, he feared, was in the process of being *digested.*

It was as if he'd been caught in a current of cold syrup, not an enjoyable feeling at all, although he could still breathe easily, and he moved without meeting any resistance. The chilly, almost clammy touch of the fluid around him did ease the hurt in his injured ankle, but otherwise it made him shudder.

Soft, blobby things drifted against him. He pushed one away and it broke open, scattering into pale white fragments. Once, as if he really were inside an enormous creature's bloodstream, he came to a place where the passage was clogged with the blob-things, and the current swirled around, but could not go anywhere. The walls bulged outward, like a balloon slowly filling.

He got out the dragon-tooth knife and cut his way through the obstruction. The current gushed forward, tumbling him slowly head over heels in a mass of white puff-balls.

He caught on to something solid and pressed his face against it, and found himself looking through a wall from the other side, as he'd done when spying on his sister and mother that first time, but this time he looked out into a room he'd never seen before, where tall, spindly robots clanked between rows of filing cabinets in the light of a single flickering bulb that dangled from the ceiling.

There was nothing of interest there, so he turned to go, but as he did the wall membrane gave way—perhaps he had accidentally cut it with his knife—and he tumbled out into the room in a torrent of fluid, which sent him swirling and spinning across the floor against a row of filing cabinets, until he hit with a thunk and banged his head, hard enough that he just sat there in a daze.

The rapidly congealing goo—Dragon House blood, or whatever it was—poured out of the hole in the wall, then gradually diminished to a small amount splashing through every few seconds, at irregular and decreasing intervals as if in time to some distant, failing heartbeat.

One of the robots waded through, holding an armload of files, apparently too stupid to notice Edward or the mess he'd made.

He managed to stand up. His head hurt. He realized he probably had a bruise, but he wasn't seriously injured. He backed away from another robot that, like the others, didn't seem to notice him.

The floor was slippery. *He* was slippery, which made the going difficult.

He couldn't get back into the hole in the wall. More robots had gathered around it and one of them sprayed the opening with something, sealing it up.

Overhead a red light had come on, blinking. He heard the faint throbbing of an alarm somewhere far off.

He backed away, slipping along, catching hold of the handles of the file drawers to steady himself until he got beyond the slime-spill and realized he was walking on the same gritty, peeling linoleum that had been on the floor of Mrs. Morgentod's "schoolroom."

Not good.

He found a door and opened it. It was a closet, filled with mops and brooms and brushes, with another dirty orange jumpsuit hanging from a hook.

He tried another door and it was locked. He looked back and saw that the robots were still milling about aimlessly, or trying to go on with their work. One had tripped and spilled a huge pile of paper into the puddle on the floor, which made the mess even worse. Some of the others seemed dimly aware that this was not right, and they tried to pick up the papers one by one, only to get themselves plastered with the sticky sheets, until they looked like blind mummies stumbling around helplessly. One after another lost its footing, tumbled and tripped several more, which caused them to fling even more paper into the air, until the whole room seemed filled with a flailing mass of upset robots with sheets of paper randomly settling over them like snow.

But Edward had no time to stand around and appreciate their discomfiture. The red light overhead was still blinking. The alarm throbbed.

There was one robot among the others, of a slightly different, less ramshackle design. It seemed a little more determined. It was neither flailing or tumbling, and if a few pieces of paper had become glued to its legs, these didn't seem to slow it down.

It made its way through the mass of others, its single, blinking red eye turning this way and that, as if looking for Edward but without quite finding him.

Just then Edward came to a third door, turned the handle, and opened it.

He found himself in a well-lighted room, in which a single brown slab stood with rope-railings all around it, as if it were on display beneath a spotlight set in the ceiling.

The slab was a rectangle, like an enormous chocolate bar, only it smelled like tar, and embedded in it was the figure of a man in what looked like a slightly rumpled band costume or possibly a captain's uniform. His hands were raised as if to ward off something, and he had a startled look on his face. His hair, such as Edward could see it, stuck out wildly. He had large muttonchop whiskers.

Edward looked closer and then whispered, desperately afraid of the conclusion he was coming to, *"Dad?"*

Somehow he didn't think this was just an image. But he had to be sure. He stepped over the rope barrier and put his hand on the thing. It did *not* feel alive, but hard and cold and slightly sticky. The oily smell was much worse up close.

He got out his knife and started to cut away the brown material. The knife went through it easily, as if through plastic, and a couple inches under the surface the stuff became brittle, and fell off in bits.

He carved very carefully until he reached the surface of the figure's right arm. Then he whittled a little, and flicked pieces away with his fingers, and before long he had uncovered about three or four inches at the right elbow and forearm. He reached in with his finger and felt *cloth*, and beneath that, very definitely, flesh and bone.

"Dad!" he called out. "Can you hear me?"

Somewhere the alarm was still throbbing, but he didn't care.

"Dad!"

Now he worked frantically, cutting and chipping away at more of the brown stuff. He worked his way up the arm, across the chest, and then he had to restrain himself and work very carefully lest he damage the face or poke out an eye.

At last he cleared the stuff away from his father's face.

But his father wasn't breathing.

"Dad! Please, Dad! Wake up! Don't be dead!"

Now he pounded on his father's chest with his fists, and more of the brown stuff fell away. He carved frantically, removing more and more until at last, out of sheer desperation he simply pushed as hard as he could until the remains of the brown slab, Dad and all, tumbled over backwards onto the floor, dragged down the rope barriers, and cracked into hundreds of pieces.

Edward felt an instant of sheer terror. He knew that if your finger is frozen badly enough and you bump it against something, you can actually break your finger off. What if it was like that? What if he'd just broken his father to bits?

But then, very much to Edward's relief, his father gasped for breath, coughed and opened his eyes.

"Dad?"

His father sat up unsteadily, brushing himself off.

"I'm a mess," he said. Then he looked up at Edward and said, "You are too, Edward."

Of course Edward *was* very messy, completely covered from head to foot with what resembled dirty oil or rancid syrup and was probably congealing dragon blood, his hair now matted with the stuff. It was starting to stink.

Yes, a mess, but Edward had no time to think about that.

"Dad?"

THE DRAGON HOUSE | 127

"Yes Edward, it's me."

"I got you out of…that." Edward waved his knife to indicate the remains of the brown slab.

"Yes, yes," his father said. "Nasty business. I saw that happen to a guy in a movie once. I don't remember how he got out of it."

Edward held up his knife.

His father looked at the knife, and was silent for a moment.

"So, it's come to that already."

"Miss Emily gave it to me. She said I had to go be a hero."

Dad lurched to his feet. He reached out with one hand and Edward caught hold to steady him.

"I am really sorry, Son, that everything has happened so quickly. It wasn't supposed to, you know."

Edward did not understand entirely what his father was talking about, but still he said, "Yeah, I know."

The alarm was definitely louder now. There were metallic footsteps in the corridor outside.

Suddenly the door burst open and in came three of the more competent sort of robot, with single, pulsating red eyes. In their hands they held what distinctly looked like guns of some sort.

"Violation! Violation! Trespass!" the three of them said in unison.

The foremost one focussed on Edward and his father.

"You are under arrest. Cease and desist. You must come with us."

Edward pointed with his knife, but didn't think it would do him much good.

Then his father took over. Confidently, he stepped forward and said, "Officer, I appreciate your concern, but there has been a misunderstanding."

Before the robot could react, Dad had draped his arm over its shoulders in a friendly way.

"I think you've misplaced something. This is what you're looking for." With a smooth motion he seemed to pull something out of the side of the robot's head, like in the magic trick, where a coin seems to appear out of someone's ear, even though the robots didn't have ears.

Dad held up what looked like a ping-pong ball.

"Your brain, isn't it?"

The robot swivelled its head from side to side uncertainly.

"Your colleagues, too, are missing a bit in the cerebral department."

He reached over and produced two more balls from the heads of the other two robots.

"Now watch."

They watched, raising and lowering their heads on telescoping necks as Dad juggled the three balls.

Then suddenly there were no balls. They'd disappeared.

The three robots pointed their guns.

"Game over. Come with us," said the leader.

"Not quite," Dad said. "I think your brains have become overheated. They're about to explode."

All three robots cocked their weapons, but before they could fire, their heads exploded like Roman candles on the Fourth of July, spraying a fountain of sparks onto the floor for several minutes. When they finally burned out, the three almost headless, smoking robots stood motionless.

Dad poked the leader with his finger and it fell over, taking the other two down with it, crashing to the floor. Bits scattered and rolled in all directions.

Dad bowed, like a stage magician at the end of his act.

"You may applaud, now, Edward. Wasn't that neat?"

Edward slipped his knife back into its sheath and, hesitatingly, clapped his hands. "Yeah, Dad, it was neat. How did you do it?"

"Well, I may not have conducted myself very competently in the past few days, I admit, but I do still know a few useful tricks. In a word: magic."

The alarm still throbbed. Something else was moving in the corridor outside.

"Do you know how to get us out of here?" Edward said.

"Point well taken."

They both started to move toward the back of the room. Then Dad paused and said, "Edward, you're limping. Did you hurt yourself?"

"Yes, Dad, I did. I'll get it looked at when this is all over. By a real doctor."

"The Dragon will heal you, Son. Reach his heart and he will make you well."

"Yeah, people have been telling me that. But first we've gotta get out of this room. How do we do that, Dad?"

His father had stopped. The point was obvious. The room had no door other than the one through which Edward had come in. Outside in the corridor, the alarm was blaring now, and many footsteps were approaching, the tread heavy, almost thundering, and perfectly in time. In addition, there was a lighter, quicker, but equally relentless step, and a voice he knew all too well.

"Edward Longstretch! I've had quite enough of your nonsense! You have been a very, very disobedient boy!"

He heard Mrs. Morgentod's schoolroom pointer banging on the sides of filing cabinets and against disabled robots, *thwack! thwack! clang!*

"Dad!" Edward shouted. "We have to get out of here! Do something!"

All the while Edward ran his hands over the walls, looking for a secret passage or a latch or something. His father meanwhile stood there, fluttering his hands in the air, snapping his fingers, and muttering, "Alakazam! Alakzoowie!"

A few motes of light floated in the air in front of him, but they didn't seem good for anything.

Edward had to come up with an idea by himself. He noticed—more felt beneath the soles of his feet than concluded intellectually—that the floor was that same curling, cheap linoleum the Department of Evil seemed to use everywhere.

It was very easy to grab hold of the edge of a square tile and yank it loose. And another. And another. He knelt down and started ripping tiles away as fast as he could, throwing them into the air. After a few seconds, Dad seemed to notice what he was doing and helped him.

They cleared an area about three feet by three feet. More than enough. Below was more of the black, tarry stuff. Edward got out his knife and started digging furiously. Both of them heaved handsful of the stuff off to the side.

Then Edward's knife hit something else, and he felt a sharp pain, as if he'd just pricked himself with a pin.

The flesh of the dragon, still alive under all that.

He cleared away as much debris as he could.

He slid his hand through.

"Go Edward," his father said. "Go now. You know what you have to do."

"What about you?"

"I'll create a diversion."

"Mom said that too the last time I saw her. I'm not sure—"

"You've seen your mother? Why didn't you say so? Well, we're in a hurry. You can tell me about it later. Trust me, Edward. If she can create a diversion, so can I. She has her peculiar talents, and I have mine."

"Dad!"

His father took him by the hand. "I'll be okay, Son."

For an instant Edward forgot everything except that he had just found his father and was about to lose him again. He stood up and hugged his father. He clung to him tearfully, but his father peeled him off and only glanced for half a second at the black, tarry smear Edward had just made all over the front of his uniform.

"No time for goodbyes, Edward," Dad said, *"You have to go!"*

The door banged open. Mrs. Morgentod screamed, "Stop right there!" and guns started going off.

Dad bent Edward over and shoved him head-first through the floor, quite roughly. This was probably necessary. They hadn't cleared away quite enough of the black stuff. For Edward it was like being hurled through a panel of rotten, flimsy plywood. There was something there, but it gave way at once and he was falling free.

For an instant, he could still hear what was going on in the room.

He heard his father say, "Good evening, Madame. Pick a card, any card."

Chapter Thirteen
The Avatar

Edward was falling through space, but slowly, almost like flying. For a moment he lacked even a sense of up and down, but that came to him, and his eyes adjusted to the darkness, and he could see, far *below* him, something glowing, a point of light or the mouth of a very long tunnel seen from far inside.

He was falling down, toward that mouth, through something that wasn't quite a fluid and wasn't quite air, thick enough for him to feel it and smell it—tarry, sooty, unpleasant enough to make him gag and to make his eyes water—and yet he could still breathe.

He could only conclude that this was one of the most damaged, polluted parts of the House, where the enemy was the strongest.

It was like descending through an enormous, gloomy cavern, miles long, and only very gradually did he realize that the rough masses covering surface of the walls were *alive,* and stirring slightly as he passed.

Fluttering their black wings, a few of them looking up from their feasting as they sucked the life out of the Dragon House.

The cavern walls were covered, as far as he could see, by *millions* of Ghastly Horrors, gathered like parasitic bats.

He could only descend quietly. He tried to swim along faster, but any motion he made had no effect on his progress.

He put his hand on his knife, to reassure himself that it was still there, but he knew that if the Horrors decided to make an extra snack out of *him* the knife wouldn't help him very much. He felt as if he were tiptoeing through a hornet hive, trying not to get stung.

Then directions seemed to shift again, and he was *rising* toward the light. He saw it as a circle that rippled slightly as if seen from beneath water.

Then he burst through the surface of what might have been water, but black, oily, dirty water, and he was looking up at a dark, but gleaming ceiling made out of some kind of crystal or metal. It was arched and vaulted, like the inside of a cathedral, and lit by balls of fire that hovered in the far recesses.

And he heard music, deep, thundering organ music, playing a familiar Halloween music that he knew very well but couldn't name: DA-DA-DA! DA-DA-DA—DA!

He swam toward the sound, and climbed up onto a ledge of some sort, then caught hold of a railing and found himself at the base of a long flight of spiral stairs. At the top of the stairs, halfway up to the ceiling was an enormous platform or balcony, where a hunched figure in a hooded black cloak played furiously on a vast pipe organ, the likes of which in all its exaggerated magnificence Edward had only seen in movies, never in real life.

As he climbed the stairs, the stones felt like just stones beneath his bare feet, not alive, not a part of the flesh of the Dragon House. As he drew near to the top he saw that the pipes of the organ were fantastically shaped out of metal into the semblance of hundreds of wriggling, serpentine dragons. But he knew they were not alive either.

The organist's playing rose to a mad crescendo, then ended with a bang of thunder that hit Edward like a physical thing and nearly sent him tumbling back down the stairs. He staggered, deafened, and it was only after a minute that he recovered and realized that the cloaked figure had risen from the organ bench and turned to greet him.

Edward came to the top of the stairs. He placed one foot, then the other very cautiously onto the polished wooden floor of the organ-loft. The wood, too, did not feel alive, at least not to him. He could not feel the presence of the Dragon House through it.

"Hello Edward," said the other, who came forward to greet him, "How good of you to drop by."

Edward backed away, just careful enough not to fall back down the stairs. He caught hold of a railing and held on tightly.

He drew his knife.

The thing before him seemed half reptilian, half human. The face was *almost* a man's face, but the eyes were too deep beneath sharp ridges, and they seemed to burn from within with red fire, and the skin was absolutely *black*, not a human color at all, but the color of dirty metal, and possibly covered with tiny scales. There was something wrong with the shape of the face that he couldn't quite definite and didn't have time to consider.

The other smiled, revealing a dripping red mouth and needle teeth.

"Edward, don't you recognize me?"

"Should…should I?"

Now the other approached him, lurching as if walking on stilts beneath its flowing black robe.

"Yes." The voice was more of a hiss now. "You should, because, you see, Edward, I am *you.*"

Now Edward began to edge his way along the railing, thinking that maybe coming up here hadn't been such a great idea after all, and maybe he should retreat down the stairs. Chances were, if the thing moved as clumsily as it seemed to, it wouldn't be very good on stairs.

"What do you mean…?"

"*I am the Avatar of the Dragon, Edward.* I think you know what that means. I think you know that dragons are more than magical beings; they are *unworldly* in a very literal sense, being not entirely part of the continuum or reality or dimension or whatever you want to call it in which we presently reside. Therefore they are seen in their true forms but rarely, by visionaries and madmen and heroes. Especially when the dragon is resting or asleep and *dreaming*, Edward—for you know that dragons dream a great deal, and very possibly you are part of a dragon's dream—*especially* when they are in such a state, they appear to be what mortal eyes take them for, assuming the shape of the skyline of an old town, or a castle, or a row of stones along a mountain ridge. *But you know all this, Edward,* and you know too that a dragon, when it is wide awake and active, when it can fight in strange wars and devour whole worlds, must have an *avatar,* a living manifestation of itself, flesh of its flesh, but in a different form, in many forms, *to which the dragon gives birth*, such as, for example, my humble self."

With this the creature made a very human gesture, a shrug, and it outspread its hands as if to say, *So, what can anybody do?* But Edward could see that its hands were entirely too large for a human being, the fingers long and thin, with several extra joints, tipped with claws, and *shrivelled*, skeletal, the metallic skin stretched tight over the long bones. He saw that the creature's neck was like that too. The vertebrae stuck out like rivets. Possibly some of the black was flaking, like rust or peeling paint. He didn't think this thing was even alive. It was a *zombie* creature, the animated *corpse* of a dragon, and he understood perfectly well what it was.

It was the spirit or avatar or manifestation of the black dragon house, the *dead* one.

Either it was wearing something like a breast-plate, or else that was just its exposed chest, black, flaking, scaled.

The creature reached for him with both claws.

"You're no avatar of *my* dragon!" Edward screamed and lunged forward, ramming his knife deep into the scaly chest.

The knife went in all the way to the hilt. The hilt hit with an audible *thunk!*

But then nothing happened. The Avatar just stood there. Edward stood there. The knife blade slid out of the wound, still in Edward's hand, and black dust and several wriggling things that might have been beetles poured out onto the floor. It was as if he'd just stabbed a sandbag, only the sandbag was animate and didn't seem much bothered.

As Edward backed away, stupefied, the Avatar of the Black Dragon stared at the wound and caught some of the dust and beetles in its hand, allowing them to dribble through its fingers.

"How very...*mythic*. Now let me get this straight, Edward. The archetypal *hero* dressed, or perhaps I should say undressed, like a junior-high reject from a barbarian comic book, travels through Mystical Realms, survives many trials, is helped along by supernatural allies, until he can stick a pointy thing in the Big Bad Big Bad...and then! Presto! From this single symbolic act all mankind is redeemed, the world is renewed, our pint-sized, barely-adolescent savior brings the gift of awesome cosmic wisdom back to his tribe, all very Thousand Faces, Joseph Campbell, Power of Myth, yadda-yadda-yadda... *is that what you have in mind, Edward?*"

And Edward, who had actually watched parts of the *Power of Myth* series on TV and had some idea what the Black Dragon's Avatar was talking about, now felt completely helpless, as if he'd been caught doing something he shouldn't have and was completely out of excuses. He couldn't think of anything better to do than nod slightly and say, "Kind of…"

With surprising speed and agility, the Avatar struck out with the back of one claw and *swatted* Edward off his feet, sending him sprawling, not toward the stairs, but under the organ, where he crashed among some pipes and levers.

The Avatar grabbed him, hard, by both legs and hauled him out of there.

"Well it *doesn't work like that, kiddo!* No, not at all. That's *right*, Edward," it said. "*I know what you are thinking*, by the way. You and I draw ever closer. It is exactly as you have feared. *Your* goody-goody dragon house has been *swallowed* by, yes, none other than yours truly, the Big Bad Big Bad, and it is rapidly being assimilated, or, you might say, *digested*. When this process is complete, no further resistance will be possible. It won't be necessary to keep you under control Edward, because that's when *I get to eat you,* and you, Edward, diminish and diminish and diminish…yum-yum, eat-him-up…into an avatar within an avatar, a tiny compartment of *my* brain where all that is left of Edward Eusebius Longstretch is kept in a little cage, and I can let you out or play with you whenever I like… and I like to play…"

It said quite a lot more which Edward didn't necessarily hear, as he lay there on the floor of the organ loft, stunned, unable to move, wondering where his knife was and slowly realizing that he'd fallen on it and it was sticking in his own chest, but at a shallow angle, ripping a huge gash from just below the collar bone, down his ribs on one side, and leaving a trail of blood across the floor where he'd been dragged.

He lay still, sobbing softly.

Something cold and hard and sharp, the avatar's clawed foot, prodded his side. He knew it could have disemboweled him with one kick if it cared to.

"…Edward, you're not paying attention. But never mind that, the rest of it will doubtless be explained to you in the course of your *training* by…my dear *wife*, whom you have already met."

Then he was poked again, by a metal-tipped wooden schoolroom pointer with which he was already well acquainted.

"Hello Edward," said Mrs. Morgentod.

He didn't know where she had come from. He didn't care. Maybe there was a trapdoor somewhere. Maybe the Black Dragon's Avatar just belched her out of his needle-toothed mouth along with a few extra bugs.

"I'm a Missus, Edward. You didn't think I was a *widow*, did you? The Avatar is part of the Dragon, yes, like a limb, but it also has considerable independent existence. It can even marry. I have the honor. We make such an excellent team."

"I don't care. You can go to Hell," Edward muttered.

Thwack! The pointer hit him hard across the back of his legs. It hurt terribly.

"That wasn't very nice, Edward. I am afraid you have not learned to be *nice*."

He took hold of his knife. He tried to get up.

Thwack! Thwack! Thwack! She hit him again, across the back, then across the shoulders, and once over the head until blood splashed into his eyes and he could hardly see. Still he crawled away from her, dragging the knife, trying to find the strength to get up.

"Edward," said the Avatar, hissing. "You can't run away. You can't fight. A real live *hero* might be able to rise up, bloodied but his spirit unbroken, and swing his mighty blade, lop off heads, and smite his way to victory—but you're not a hero, Edward. You're some dumb little kid who isn't going to amount to much of anything except, ultimately, my breakfast."

Edward managed to force himself to his hands and knees, but the Avatar kicked him in the ribs, just hard enough to send him sprawling, like a cat playing with a wounded mouse.

He tried to crawl under the organ again, but Mrs. Morgentod hit him very hard indeed, right on his injured ankle. He rolled over, sobbing.

The Avatar crouched down, grabbed him by the hair, and yanked him around. It spoke, its needle teeth inches from his face. It had a breath like car exhaust.

"I don't get to eat you right away, Edward, at least not *all* of you right away. Maybe a bit here, a bit there, as my dear wife, your *keeper*, instructs you in your duties, as you *work for us,* cooperating *fully* while we make use of, then ultimately dismantle your dragon, your life, and your world. And then…boo-hoo!…sob, after your Mommy and your Daddy and Big Sister and everybody you ever knew is *dead* and the planet Earth is a cold, black slag heap rolling through space, *then* you are of no more use to us and I get to eat you. But in the meantime…"

One clawed finger scraped across his cheek. Edward tried to turn away.

The Avatar yanked his head around to face it.

"…but in the meantime, Edward, I thought I would have a little snack, and take your eyes and gobble them down. You'd probably be more useful to us blind anyway."

"Definitely more docile," said Mrs. Morgentod. "Do it."

Edward screamed. He slashed again with his knife, not trying to stab the Avatar, which he knew would be useless, much less cut off its hand, which would be likely.

What he did instead was cut through his own hair. Possibly on some sub-rational level he realized that if he'd been wearing a buzz cut the fate of the entire universe would have been quite different, but fortunately his hair was rather long, so he was able to cut himself free in one stroke, leaving the Avatar holding a handful of it, then roll away.

Thwack! Mrs. Morgentod's pointer hit the floor right where Edward's head had just been, then missed again as he lurched to his feet.

He felt very weak, dizzy, sick. His left leg didn't seem to want to work at all. The ankle seemed to fold under him. He realized that he was probably quite badly hurt. The pain was getting worse by the second. He could hop on his right foot, waving his arms to maintain a precarious balance.

But somehow he knew what to do. A voice deep within himself, the voice of an *other* with which he had an *affinity* spoke to him, said *Edward, come to me, Edward. Come into my heart.*

Knowing what to do, he used his knife to cut the palm of his right hand, as American Natives do, at least in stories, when they want to swear blood-brotherhood.

He held up his bleeding hand and shouted, "Dragon! Take my blood!"

Then, before the Black Dragon's Avatar or Mrs. Morgentod could stop him, he half leapt, half tumbled over the railing of the organ-loft, out into space, whether to his death or to something else, he was no longer in any condition to care.

Chapter Fourteen
The Heart of the Dragon

He was soaring again. Up and down seemed confused. Before him, below him, was the surface of the lake from which he had emerged. Now flames roared on its surface. All around him, Ghastly Horrors shrieked, detached themselves from the walls, and hurled after him, but could not catch him.

He splashed through. The Ghastly Horrors, striking all round him, burst into flame, then dissipated into smoke.

Edward sank down, deep, beneath the House, into the depths of the Dragon itself, as he had done only once before. Now he was returning, as if from memory, into an interrupted dream.

He found himself, once more, inside a vast, stony cavern. He wasn't entirely sure how he'd gotten there. He knew he was hurt. He wasn't thinking all that clearly.

For a moment he just lay on his back, on the rough, damp stones, enjoying the cool sensation. The air itself was very cold. He began to shiver. But he hurt a bit less.

Edward.

The voice was more in his mind than something he heard through his ears.

He rolled over on the cold stone, dirt and pebbles shifting against his bare skin. He looked up. He had to push his hair out of his face. It had been plastered to his forehead with blood.

He saw before him, floating in the darkness, the two eyes of the Dragon, *his* Dragon, the eyes of the Dragon House itself. They were fainter than he had seen them before, giving off very little light, very difficult to see but definitely there.

Edward, you and I are one being now. You must come to me, into me. Your blood must renew my heart.

He thought it was something like that, though he didn't fully understand. He tried to get to his feet, but with a suddenly stab of pain, his left ankle *did* fold under him, and with a gasp, he dropped to his knees. He banged one knee as he did.

He knew what he had to do. First he tried hopping on his right leg again, balancing himself with his outstretched arms, but, barefoot on rough, irregular stones, that didn't work very well, and he fell again, hurting the knee again, and an elbow.

He had to crawl, slowly, with great effort, all the while holding his left hand, the one he had slashed with the knife, in a tight fist.

Did he still have the knife? Yes, he did, in his right hand. He held that, too, in a fist, and in this clumsy way made his way toward the eyes of the Dragon.

When he drew near, the stones before him shifted and fell away in little avalanches of stone, and side of the cavern opened up to become the mouth of the Dragon.

Edward...

He kept on going. It wasn't merely as if he were crawling into a cave or tunnel. His blood touched the Dragon. He *was* the Dragon. His senses became divided, so he was crawling, cold, rather badly banged up, still in a good deal of pain, over rough stones. At the same time he felt as if he were lying in space, floating, while something very small and warm crawled or slid down his throat.

In the tunnel, in the Dragon's mouth, he tried to stand one more time, but the pain was too great. He nearly fainted. There was no doubt that his left ankle was broken.

The Dragon sighed in its half-dreaming state. Warm breath washed over Edward. He felt a little better. He continued on his way.

He also felt, in a distant, abstract way, what the Dragon felt, the horrible sensation of millions of Ghastly Horrors devouring its flesh and drinking its blood, like being slowly eaten alive by maggots.

The Dragon itself was fading. It too, like Edward, could not really form coherent thoughts. It called his name. He struggled on. Because they were flesh of one flesh, of an *affinity* as he had been told so many times by now, he was able to slide into the Dragon, to sink into it, to make his way into its bloodstream, toward the heart.

Edward felt something warm moving inside his chest.

He came to a place of golden light. His eyes were dazzled. He heard something beating, like a vast, muffled drum, *thump-thump, thump-thump,* only less and less regular, the beats weaker and weaker. Nevertheless, within the room of golden light, when he could somehow see again, squinting into the glare, he beheld before him what might have been a king seated on a luminous throne; but it was not a king, instead a half-human, half dragon figure draped in a golden robe.

Edward realized that the human part of the face was a boy's face. It was his own. His features were, at the same time, shifted and changed, and his face was the face of a dragon.

The seated figure reached out with its left hand, which, Edward saw, was slashed and bleeding. Edward clasped it with his own left hand, and his blood and that of the other mingled; and there was no difference at all between them. The *thump-thump* of the Dragon's heartbeat steadied.

Then there was only golden light again, and Edward felt himself floating in a warm space. He felt his body, his *vast* dragon body stir and begin to awaken. He felt the millions of parasites which afflicted him, the Ghastly Horrors, flutter in alarm.

Edward, at the same time found himself back in the stony cavern, lying nearly naked in the cold, damp air.

It felt good.

He stood up. His ankle didn't hurt him anymore.

He knew what he had to do.

Knife in hand, he dove *into the stones* and passed through the floor of the cavern.

The Dragon, which was also Edward, began to move. It rushed forward like an express train, crashing through the inside of the Black Dragon which had swallowed it, smashing through rotting structures, an avalanche of stone and wood and metal crashing down upon it but not slowing it in the least. Robots waved their limbs helplessly and were crushed. Minions, human and otherwise, scattered. Ghastly Horrors took flight in great clouds, exploding into noxious dust when the Dragon burst through the mass of them.

Edward, who was also the Dragon, drifted upward through stone, downward, sideways; all sense of direction was lost, confused, but he felt the earth and stone around him *lessen*, and then he emerged, like a diver breaking the surface of a lake, through the smooth floor at the base of the stairs, below the organ-loft.

The actual "lake" before him was drained now. The Avatar and

Mrs. Morgentod stood overseeing a vast operation. Thousands of minions, some of them more or less human, some half-reptile, some with wings and the trumpet-faces of Ghastly Horrors, labored to dig out the bottom of the lake. They had earth-moving equipment, a bulldozer and several back-hoes.

"Where is that damned *brat?*" said Mrs. Morgentod. "Find him! Find him!"

"Are you looking for me?" said Edward, coming up behind them.

Mrs. Morgentod whirled about and shrieked, her cry deafening and indescribably hideous. Indeed, the sound of it hit Edward like a physical blow and staggered him back. Then she was shouting something else, a series of words, an incantation or a command, and he couldn't hear it.

But his strength now was considerably more than just the physical strength of a boy who weighed about a hundred pounds and had never been any good in gym class. He and the Dragon were one. His strength was that of the Dragon.

He caught the downstroke of her pointer with the blade of his knife, parried, and heaved her away. She came at him again, and he blocked her again.

The whole cavern shook, as in an earthquake. The organ, overhead, began to collapse into itself, pipes shrieking.

The Dragon, which was Edward, was locked in a desperate struggle with the Black Dragon, which was a dead thing, filled with millions of squirming, vile creatures. The Dragon, the true Dragon, which was Edward, was at least alive. It was not at full strength, quite weak by dragon standards, but it had the advantage of being *alive,* capable of coordinated movement, while the other thing was simply a hulking, blundering mass.

The true Dragon breathed fire. The body of the black, dead thing which imprisoned it began to burn, to peel away.

Edward, who was the Dragon, struggled with Mrs. Morgentod by the shore of the vast, empty lake, while the earthquake continued, stones rained down from above, and the assorted minions abandoned their work and began to scatter.

The Dragon, which was Edward, roared, spewing fire. It cut its way free from all encumbrance. Darkness loomed ahead, a darkness filled with stars.

The Black Dragon's Avatar, on the edge of the empty lake, rendered no assistance whatsoever to Mrs. Morgentod. It made several clicking sounds, lurched about like a drunk on stilts, and then began to collapse into itself. Its head sank down into its chest. Smoke poured out of numerous openings in its body. It crumbled, twitching, into a smoldering heap.

Mrs. Morgentod shrieked once more. She could temporarily deafen Edward, but she couldn't stop him. As he experienced the combat, it was in silence, almost like a dance. He parried her blows again and again.

The Dragon, which was Edward, broke into open space above a greenish blue, striped planet with three moons overhead and several more lower down by the horizon. The Dragon shook itself, like a dog emerging from water, scattering the remains of the dead thing which had enclosed it.

It spread its wings and soared.

Edward, who was the Dragon, caught Mrs. Morgentod's pointer with his left hand and snatched it from her grasp. With his right, wielding the knife, he struck off her head in a single blow.

Her body dropped to hands and knees, groping around for the head.

The head tried to scream, but, lacking lungs, couldn't. Its jaw worked furiously, as if to yell to the body, *Hey, over here, stupid! Over here!*

Now Edward sheathed his knife and took the pointer in both hands by the tip, which was narrower than the handle. Although he had never played golf in his life, and had no interest in golf, he nevertheless executed an absolutely perfect golf swing and sent Mrs. Morgentod's head sailing out, out over the vast empty lake, into the darkness beyond.

Edward wasn't sure where it went, but he knew he'd hit a hole in one.

The Dragon, pulling away from the striped planet, coughed out a cloud of black smoke and bits of debris.

Edward hawked and spat, as if he'd just coughed up something small and hard and foul-tasting.

Beside him, the headless body of Mrs. Morgentod groped about. It caught hold of his ankles.

"No," he said. "Oh no you don't!"

He drove the tip of the point right where Mrs. Morgentod wouldn't ever want it, through her back between the shoulderblades, and out the other side.

He really wished his sister Margaret could be here, to help him do this. She'd wanted to, so very much.

The pointer would have pierced Mrs. Morgentod's heart, if she'd had one.

Of that Edward could never be sure. The body was light and stiff and fragile, like something made of papier-mache.

After a while it was more like ash.

* * * *

What followed for Edward was more like a dream. He was just Edward, now. The Dragon's strength receded from him, like a hand withdrawn from a glove, and he was just a boy again, wearing only a dragon-skin loincloth, with a knife stuck in the waist.

Somehow he was no longer on the ledge overlooking the empty lake bed scattered with abandoned earth-moving equipment and squashed minions. That scene blurred and was gone, like something erased when you shake an Etch-a-Sketch.

He was swimming through the walls of the Dragon House. It was as easy as moving his own hand or arm. He floated up, into warm light. It was very pleasant. He could just lie still, and rise into the light. He rippled through the walls. He looked out into rooms he had never seen before, and some that he recognized. The carousel turned slowly, but steadily. It was still covered with dust.

He passed along the ceiling of the kitchen. Most of the dishes had been flung from the cabinets and smashed.

At the very last, he pushed his way gently out from old-fashioned wallpaper, into a bedroom he recognized.

Someone turned suddenly and said, "Oh, Sir!"

He fell into the arms of Miss Emily Armitage. He was not particularly in any pain, but he felt very weak, exhausted beyond anything he'd ever imagined possible. He slid down to his knees.

She caught him under the arms and lifted him up.

"No, no," she said. "I should kneel to you!"

And she did, leaving him swaying before her, quite confused.

He wasn't sure he liked being treated this way.

"Why are you—?"

"Oh, Edward, don't you understand what you have done, what you have become? You are now the *Avatar*!"

He recoiled from her for a moment in shock, trying to make sense of all this. He just couldn't. He caught hold of a bedpost and stood there, swaying, clinging desperately so he wouldn't fall.

Suddenly Miss Emily was fluttering everywhere at once. At first she seemed to be trying to pack things of her own into a bag, as if she suddenly had to vacate the room. But then she rushed back to him, and waved her hands uncertainly, and ran toward the door, then came back.

"Oh, Edward, Edward. You have to come with me. You're the hero. You're the master of the House now. You've saved the day. Everyone wants to meet you. There will be a banquet in your honor."

"Everyone?"

"Oh, I don't know. Everyone. Dignitaries, presidents, professors, mucketty-a-mucks. They'll probably want to pin a medal on you."

Edward could just imagine them trying to pin a medal on his bare chest.

He was supposed to go meet—*who*?

Here he was, wearing almost nothing, still covered head to foot in oil, ash, dried blood, dirt, fragments of Ghastly Horrors, and who knew what else. He couldn't even tell what kind of condition he was in under all that. He was aware that he smelled pretty bad. Miss Emily didn't seem to have noticed yet that he'd left a smear down the front of her dress when he embraced her, even as he'd done to his father's uniform.

"No!" he said. "No! No! I'm all *yucky*! I'm not going anywhere until I get a *bath*!"

"Why of course, dearie," said Miss Emily.

Chapter Fifteen

The Most Wonderful Bath in the History of the Universe and What Followed After

It was the most wonderful bath in the history of the universe, Edward decided after about two seconds. The bathroom, which seemed a bit larger and more elaborately furnished than it had been the last time he'd seen it, was thick with welcoming steam. The tub was a huge, marble affair, with dragon legs, which very possibly wriggled their claws slightly against the floor as he came into the room, but he wasn't sure about that. The faucets were gold, and shaped like dragon-mouths.

He undid his loincloth and let his knife drop to the floor, then slid into the warm water beneath a layer of thick bubbles. He let himself sink all the way down, and ran his fingers through his hair and rubbed his scalp, to get the unbelievable amounts of gunk out of his hair.

He only bobbed to the surface when he finally had to breathe. Then he lay with his head against the back of the tub and with his arms draped over the side to keep himself steady, in perfect comfort, wishing that this moment would never go away.

It must have been a miraculous aspect of the tub that no matter how much ash, oil, blood, and slime came off him, the water still seemed perfectly clean. It bubbled gently, like in a jacuzzi.

At one point a large rubber duck bobbed to the surface and said, "Is everything to your satisfaction, Edward?"

"Oh yes," he said, half asleep. "Everything's fine."

Still he lay there, letting himself float. Nothing hurt anywhere. He raised his left leg out of the water and turned his foot this way and that, realizing that his ankle wasn't broken anymore, although he had a pale scar all the way around, another on his right ankle, and a much larger one, jagged like a lightning bolt, across his chest. There was still another, tear-shaped and about the size of a quarter on his right thigh, from where he'd gotten cut on a branch falling through the trees. He also found a very thin, pale line across his left palm, from where he had mingled his blood with that of the Dragon.

He had some vague idea that a proper, conquering hero probably should have a few battle scars, and that he'd earned these honorably, but he could not hold the thought. He also discovered that the golden dragon scale he wore around his neck had become part of him. The chain was gone, his fingers told him, but the scale itself had melted into his skin just below the collar bone and felt a little like a very thick callus, hard, but flexible, giving no discomfort as he touched it.

He didn't think much about that either. He just wanted to lie here forever, floating amid the warm suds, and forget about the world and all his adventures. So he did, for at least an hour, or even more. The water never grew cold.

But eventually the rubber duck said, "Hey, lazybones. They really *are* waiting for you downstairs."

In defiance he dropped below the surface and blew bubbles, but then came up for breath.

"Out, out," said the duck. "Get moving."

Edward glared.

"With all due respect, sir," said the duck.

As if to enforce the point, the tub began to drain.

Edward climbed out and dried himself, a little unsteady on his feet almost as if he had been floating for so long that he had to get reacquainted with gravity. Also, he was very, very tired. He really just wanted to go to bed, but I supposed he'd better go downstairs if all those people were waiting for him.

He wasn't sure who exactly. He wasn't sure either how they had come together so quickly, but then the passage of time inside the Dragon House didn't always make sense. How long had he been in the caverns confronting the evil Avatar? How long had it taken him to come back? What might have seemed minutes down there might have been days up here.

Wrapped in the towel, he stumbled back into the bedroom. He didn't see Miss Emily anywhere. Furthermore, it wasn't her bedroom anymore, but something much larger and grander. There was a four-post bed with a canopy over it, and lots of furniture he'd never seen before, and glass-covered shelves filled with books, tapestries, drapery, several strange lamps, what looked like skulls, and stuffed specimens of various sorts that he couldn't identify, and much more. Now there was a large, bay window, through which he saw black sky, and seemingly motionless stars.

As he was taking all this in, his foot suddenly slid out from under him and he only recovered by catching hold of the back of a chair. He realized, to his surprise that he'd nearly tripped over Mrs. Morgantod's pointer, which lay on the floor, perhaps where he'd unknowingly carried it and dropped it, or else where it had somehow floated to the surface at the conclusion of the battle below.

He picked up the pointer and hefted it. It didn't seem all that heavy now, just a metal-tipped stick. But he thought he should keep it as a trophy, and sure enough, on a blank section of the wall there were two hooks ready to hold it.

He thought for a moment, only half-seriously, about having her head mounted on a plaque above that, but, no, that would never do. He didn't want her looking at him as he slept.

He didn't doubt that this was his room now. He was master of the house, as Miss Emily had told him. This was the master bedroom.

But what made it genuinely *his* was the fact that his old dresser had been brought in, and the single book case he'd had since he was very young, on which all his specimens and samples and doodads were neatly placed. His actual books were on the floor, in the boxes waiting for him to arrange them properly.

Even his Fokker Triplane was there, on top of the book-case. It was still broken, but it and all the loose pieces had been placed carefully in a large bowl, and a tube of glue, tweezers, and an exacto-knife were lined up neatly beside it.

The first thing he did was open the dresser and quickly put on a t-shirt and cut-off shorts, because they were *his* and familiar and comfortable, but then he realized that if he was going to meet famous people or dignitaries or whoever they were, maybe he should dress better than that.

He opened the walk-in wardrobe nearby and then stepped back, amazed. It seemed to go on forever. Right in front of him, hung neatly on a hanger, was a leopard skin. It was the sort that Tarzan might favor, though of the more modest type that draped over one shoulder (jungle formal-wear, perhaps). Next to it, he saw a uniform fit for Napoleon, complete with hat; a tuxedo; a cowboy outfit with furry chaps and a ten-gallon Stetson; a Roman toga; a jester suit with stripes, motley, and bells; a set of buckskins, with feathers; neatly-pressed slacks, shirt, coat and tie such as a prep-school kid might wear (but Edward didn't like ties and barely knew how to tie one); and, in fact, every conceivable kind of clothing, costume or outfit that he could imagine, and several he had *not* imagined and couldn't entirely make sense out of. A spacesuit stood in one corner, medieval armor in another. Inevitably, everything was in his size.

Then he found what he was looking for. Instinctively, he knew this was right: a magician's gown, a little like a Chinese emperor's robe, of dark blue silk, with dragons and stars embroidered on it in gold. This virtually slid over him, and fit loosely, billowing as he moved. Its touch was smooth and slightly cool. He noticed, standing before a mirror, that the robe somehow rippled as he walked, completely covering his feet, but never tripping him, and concealing the motion of his legs so that he seemed to *glide* along the floor like a ghost, in absolute silence. It was a really neat effect. He liked it quite a lot.

Then there was the question of footwear. He had a choice of everything from sneakers to winged sandals to cowboy boots with spurs—and there actually *was* a pair of large, white, exceedingly fluffy bunny-rabbit slippers.

But as he stood there barefoot on the polished wooden floor, he was in direct contact with the living flesh of the Dragon, which was the House, for which he had, in ways he still had not worked out entirely, a special affinity. The feeling was comforting. He didn't want to give it up.

Besides, he was Master of the Dragon House, even if he wasn't totally sure what all that entailed, so he decided it gave him permission to attend a formal banquet (or whatever) in his bare feet if he felt like it.

He went to the door. He was ready. But first he stood there, leaning against the door, letting his hand slip into the wood a little bit, even as he let his feet sink into the floor, ankle-deep.

Now he once more shared the sensations of the Dragon House. He seemed to be everywhere at once. Since they were still, apparently, in outer space, the feeling was very different than anything he'd experienced before. He felt the deep cold of space, and the heat of the sun, though neither was uncomfortable, and even the tiny particles from solar radiation—the wind from the sun—like sand blowing gently over his skin. The occasional pinging meteor was like a faint pinprick, but the silk robe seemed to absorb the sensation.

He knew now where the new arrivals were coming from. There was a ship of some sort hooked to the House's airlock. (Did the Dragon House *have* an airlock? Well, it did now.) Also, some of the newcomers just winked into existence, out of thin air.

Much more close at hand, he was aware of things moving throughout the house, living creatures and robots, already beginning to repair the mess from the recent havoc.

Closer still, he heard people talking about him in a room downstairs. Some of the voices he recognized, some he did not.

"Why do we always get the timid ones?"

"I wouldn't call Edward timid. No, that is not the correct word."

"Well, bashful then. A little ill-at-ease socially."

"We do less well with the oh-so-confident, big, muscular, booming-extrovert, jock types, anyway. They're too used to winning at everything. They haven't learned how to struggle. They tend to fold up when the going gets tough."

"He is still very young, and he wasn't prepared at all."

"I think he did very well, all things considered."

Suddenly there was a rapping on the other side of the door and Edward heard a deep voice saying, "Master, sir, it is time."

Edward stepped back, then opened the door, and saw, hunched there, one of the living stone gargoyles. He had pretty much given up on the idea of telling them apart. He supposed that if he was Master, then they were his minions. He'd never had minions before. He wasn't sure how to respond.

"Hello," he said.

"Sir," said the gargoyle, extending its hand.

"And your name is…?"

"Gargoyle, sir."

"No nicknames? Never Gargy?"

"Never, sir."

Edward allowed himself to be led down the stairs, which didn't go where they had previously, but now descended into a series of corridors lined with portraits containing figures that turned to watch him as he passed, and lighted by candlesticks held by living hands and arms.

Then he was walking on a thick, red carpet, but this too was part of the House, and he could feel the presence of the Dragon through it.

Two more gargoyles, who had been standing stiffly at attention, saluted and swung two enormous, gleaming doors open wide, revealing a ballroom, with magical lights flickering around the chandeliers as if alive.

A crowd of people, and things that were not quite people rose from around a broad table when he came in.

He walked slowly, a little intimidated by all this. He scanned the crowd for familiar faces, and was very happy to see his father, in a clean captain's uniform, his mother, dressed as a white witch, and his sister Margaret, still in the gingham dress, her hair elaborately done up in an old-fashioned style, no doubt by Miss Emily. Miss Emily herself was not at the table. She winked at him out of a portrait hanging on the wall.

He also saw Zarcon of Zarconaz, polished and looking very well, his head attached to a new, spidery body with numerous limbs, though what might be called his chest still did somewhat resemble a vacuum cleaner, and he had a suction hose.

Even the Librarian was there, along with several assistants, glowing crystal skulls atop swirls of drapery and shadow that the eye couldn't quite follow, the bones of their skeletal hands no more than thin, glowing lines, like scratches in the air.

There were many people, and beings, and devices, that he didn't recognize at all, but for all of them, he was the center of attention, the hero.

This was going to take a lot of getting used to.

Everybody seemed to be waiting for him to say something.

"But where's Doctor Basileus?" he finally asked.

"Don't worry about him," Dad said. "He's in an escape capsule, somewhere near the Moon. We should be picking him up tomorrow. He's very eager to see you, Edward."

"Oh."

"Won't you take the seat of honor, sir?" said the gargoyle that had accompanied Edward.

As he passed by his mother, she leaned toward him and whispered, "Edward, your forgot to comb your hair. It looks like a fright wig!"

"Well, boys that age always are a little untidy," someone said.

He sat in the high seat like a throne at the table. This seat *wasn't* his size. In fact he feet couldn't reach the floor, something he found alarming, but then he realized that the seat itself was alive, and he could touch the Dragon by just putting a hand on the armrest.

Maybe it had been a trick of the light. He hadn't been sure before, but *now* the table was covered with a very fine banquet. There was everything Edward had ever liked to eat, and quite a bit he had never seen before. Zarcon of Zarconax *insisted* that the roast hammaframmis *must* be eaten with fungleworp sauce, although Edward found that he liked it either way.

It was surprising that Zarcon, who seemed more machine than not, should even have an opinion, much less an appetite, but he did.

Edward realized that he *was* very hungry. When was the last time he'd eaten anything at all? Probably when he and Margaret had shared their supplies out of the grocery bag in the library, but how long ago was that?

Something for him to work out later.

There were toasts and announcements and congratulations and speeches. He *was* given a medal, but it wasn't pinned on him, instead lowered over his head on a golden, cloth band.

Everyone had questions. He tried to answer as many as he could, and told some of his adventures, as best as he could remember them, but in no coherent order, and often drifting away from the train of thought. He only became animated when he described what had happened to Mrs. Morgentod.

He looked down the table to his sister and said, "I wish you could have been there, Mags."

She laughed and said, "Yeah, me too."

The one thing that convinced him that this was all real, not some kind of dream, was the fact that Margaret still had a large, nasty bruise on her forehead, which the new hairdo and some makeup had failed to disguise.

After a while, he felt very full, and had not saved room for dessert. He was only aware of the bright lights, and that the room was very warm, but in a comfortable sort of way. The voices of the others faded to a kind of murmur, like a tide lapping against the side of a boat.

He did distinctly hear someone say, "Why do we always get the sleepy ones?"

He wasn't entirely aware that someone, probably a gargoyle, though it might have been his father, put him to bed, sorcerer's robe and all.

Now he did dream, of flying, golden dragons, rising into the bright sky, into the Sun. He was among them, one of them. For a moment his eyes were dazzled, but then he could see again, in something other than ordinary sight, and he beheld a vast, golden dragon curled inside the Sun, its coils winding and turning, its gleaming face even yet too bright for him to look upon directly.

"Welcome, Edward," it said. "And well done."

Chapter Sixteen
Family Matters

The next morning, Edward awoke, alone, in that fantastic bedroom. He sat up, still dressed in his sorcerer's robe. He slid his feet down onto the floor and felt the presence of the living House through the rug. He stood for a while, looking at the thin scar on the palm of his left hand. It wasn't that he needed any convincing that this was real and not a dream, or even that he suspected he might be *still dreaming*, but nevertheless he gazed at the mark on his hand as if it were the mysterious key to everything.

Outside the window, he saw the Earth, huge, and flattening out until he could not longer see it all at once. There was a white glow as the House entered the atmosphere.

He went down to breakfast, pleased to discover that the door out of his bedroom now led down, more or less the way it once had, into his old, wrecked room. From there he found the other flight of stairs which led to the front of the house, where he had first come in, that first night, when the family arrived.

The kitchen was where it used to be. Mom, now dressed in her daily around-the-house clothes, and Margaret, in pajamas, were waiting for him. He had a very ordinary breakfast of cereal, fruit, and juice. No one said anything for a while.

He looked at the bruise on his sister's forehead. It looked bad, but he supposed it was getting better, turning yellowish around the edges. Still, he winced to look at it.

"I'll be okay," said Margaret, noticing this. "How about you?"

Edward looked again at the scar on his hand, then said, "Me too, I guess."

"What are you going to do today?"

"Oh, I thought I'd go out in the woods some."

"You'll have to wait till we get back to Earth for that."

"We're almost there," said Edward.

Even as he spoke the house groaned and shook. The milk in his cereal bowl rippled. Then everything was still.

"I think we just arrived," said Edward.

But this wasn't going to be an ordinary day. Already he was beginning to suspect that he would never have an ordinary day again.

When he was done his breakfast, his mother took away his cereal bowl and put it in the sink. Then she sat down at the table. She wasn't smiling.

Someone came into the kitchen. Edward turned around in his chair.

It was his father, in his uniform, what Edward thought of as the Captain Nemo suit. With him, whirring slightly as he moved, was Zarcon of Zarconax, and Doctor Basileus.

Edward started to get up, but Doctor Basileus took him by the hand and said, "No need to rise on my behalf."

"I'm so glad to see you."

"I am glad to see you too, Edward. I can only apologize that I did not manage to be of much service during the recent troubles. I shall endeavor to do better in the future."

Dad fetched an extra chair for the doctor, then sat down himself. Zarcon didn't seem to need a chair. He adjusted his various legs, claws, and wheels to the correct height.

"Edward," his father said slowly, "I think it is time for you to know everything, or as much of everything as I am capable of explaining to you. I will be ably assisted, I am sure, by my two colleagues. In the course of your future studies you will learn a lot more, considerably more than I myself will ever know. But first, let me give you a choice. We can have our little talk while touring fantastic parts of the house. There's a big laboratory upstairs that you haven't seen yet, filled with bottles and bubbling vats and electrical thingies with lighting crackling all over them, like something in a movie. Or, we could all just stay here. You'll see the rest eventually anyway."

"Let's just stay here, Dad," Edward said.

"Fine. You know what this is…about…don't you?"

"Kind of."

"It's about you, Edward. Things didn't exactly go according to plan."

"I know that much, Dad."

Now there seemed to be tears in his father's eyes. That, to Edward, was both amazing and frightening.

"Edward, you weren't quite told the truth about something." His father held up his hands. He was wearing gloves. "Remember when you were told that when you're really good at it, you can touch the house even wearing gloves? Well, maybe that's true. Maybe *you* will one day be able to do it with just your pinkie, or even wearing gloves, but the implication you were given was deliberately misleading. The reason all of us keepers and watchers and custodians and the like wear gloves is so that we *won't* touch it. If we do, it reminds us of what we can *never* have and *never* do. I *can* feel the Dragon, but I can never be a *part* of it, as you can, Edward. That's because you and I different. Very different." Then Dad looked up at Mom and said, "I'm not sure how to do this."

Mom took over. "Edward," she said gently. "You know how some children often get the idea that maybe they don't really quite belong in their family, and the thing they're most afraid of is finding out that they're adopted?"

"Mom, what are you saying? Am I adopted?"

"It's a little worse than that."

"Oh Edward!" his father said. "You weren't supposed to find out that way, but you had to find out. You must have noticed the lack of family resemblance. The reason for that is that you are *not* in any normal way of speaking a member of the family at all. You are very, very different from the rest of us. You are not even, by the strictest of definitions…a human being."

"I'm not…*what*?" This made *no* sense.

Now his father was crying slightly. His voice quavered. "I am sorry, Son. It is not often that a father has to tell his son that he's not actually his son or even quite a member of the same species."

"Dad!" Edward looked from one face to another around the table. Dad was tearful. Mother was very grave. Margaret looked shocked and afraid. Zarcon's metal face was just metal. Doctor Basileus looked compassionate and wise, but a little sad.

Edward looked to him.

"Edward," said the doctor, "I think you know much about dragons by now. They come from a place we cannot see, at the center of time and the center of the universe, perhaps, or another dimension, in any case beyond the reach of human perception. They are indeed, as all peoples have suspected throughout history, extremely magical creatures. They are also nearly immortal. Perhaps they do live forever unless they are destroyed, as you recently saw one destroyed."

Edward was too bewildered to follow all this. He had seen enough and experienced enough to be willing to believe *anything* at this point, and he didn't think everyone was playing a joke on him, so what they were saying had to be more or less true, even if Dad had admitted lying about the gloves; which meant quite a few things he couldn't quite wrap his mind around just now. He'd read somewhere that sometimes, when a soldier is gravely wounded in battle, even fatally so, he will sometimes just feel a thump where the bullet went in, and be able to go on for a little while, because it takes that much time for the pain to catch up with him.

He felt like that now. He didn't know why Doctor Basileus was suddenly lecturing about dragons, but he was too numb to interrupt. He just sat there, looking at the mark in the palm of his left hand.

"…but dragons have cycles. Sometimes they go to sleep for centuries, during which time their form changes. They are camouflaged to look like mountain ranges, or castles, or large houses. You know this, Edward. What you also know something about, is that when a dragon wakes up again, when it becomes active, it produces an *avatar,* an outward manifestation of itself which, in a way, anchors it into earthly reality. A dragon with an avatar is more than a myth. It's quite solid."

As if to make the point further, Doctor Basileus tapped his foot on the floor.

Edward for once drew his own feet up, away from the floor. He sat curled up in his sorcerer's gown staring at the mark on his hand.

"Edward," Dad said. "When you reached through the wall for the very first time, what did you feel?"

"Glass jars, Dad. Big enough to be water coolers."

"You were reaching to the place of your beginning, Edward," said Doctor Basileus. "That was where you were born."

"To use the term imprecisely," said Zarcon of Zarconax.

"I made you," Dad said, "out of a drop of your mother's blood, some chemicals, and a splinter from the house. You grew like a plant inside that jar, until you looked like a baby. Then we took you out and raised you. I'm your creator, Edward, but not your father."

"I'm like…a clone then?"

"No, Edward. The correct term is *homunculus*."

Edward had some idea of what a homunculus was from reading, some gnarly mud-man grown by a medieval alchemist for weird and sinister purposes.

Edward just sat there, stunned. No one said anything for several minutes.

Finally Edward said, sobbing softly, "I feel like Pinocchio. I want to be a *real boy*."

Suddenly Dad reached over and rapped his knuckles on Edward's head. "Well you have to admit, it gives 'knock on wood' a whole new meaning!"

Edward glared at him. Dad withdrew, obviously aware that for once his joke had been desperately, awfully unfunny, and not very well timed either.

"Edward," said Doctor Basileus. "You *are* a real boy, just a very special one. None of us remembers being born. We don't see where we come from. It's a story we're told. Your story is a little different, that's all."

"You're the Avatar," Dad said. "You are part of the house."

"Yeah," said Edward bitterly. "Like a doorknob."

"It's not like that at all," said Doctor Basileus. "The one thing that Mrs. Morgentod and her husband apparently told you which is *actually true*, is that the Avatar is very much a separate being, who has a life of his or her own. You know that Miss Emily was your predecessor. The Avatar is a distinct person, and may even marry and have a family."

"She didn't."

"She didn't. That was her choice. But you, Edward, have your own choices."

"You have to study very hard," Mom cut in. "Being an Avatar of a dragon is serious work. You can't walk away from it. It is *who you are.*"

"I didn't ask to be who I am," said Edward.

Dad reached across the table and took hold of both of Edward's hands. "Look at me, Son."

But Edward just sat there limply, looking down at the tabletop.

Tears ran down his cheeks.

"Look at me!"

Edward raised his head.

Dad looked him straight in the eyes and said, "I have never been more truthful with you than I am being right now. It doesn't matter where you come from. We love you, Edward. Your mother and I both love you. We're sorry everything worked out the way it did, that everything happened so quickly. The plan was perfect. We move into this spooky old house. We live here for years and years, while you and your sister go to school and have a more or less normal life. Then, when you're grown up, after you get out of college, I take you aside and say, 'Son, now that you are of age, it's about time I tell you about the family curse.'"

"But I'm not part of the family, so it can't be a family curse."

Dad let go of one of Edward's hands and knocked on his own head.

"*I'm* the family curse, Edward. I am the one who screwed up. It seems that somebody left a window open—"

Edward looked suddenly to Margaret, who started to shake her head and say, "No, no, I'm sorry. I didn't mean it—"

"Not *that* window," Dad said. "It's *my* fault that a metaphysical guard was left down, a supernatural detail was not attended to. There will be an investigation, no doubt. I'm sure I'll be in trouble with the Agency, because, as I am sure you have figured out, Edward, your old man…if you can still think of me as your old man…"

"I don't know what to think," said Edward.

"…your old man is a bit of a goof. I have never been very good at what I do. Remember how many times I tried to do a magic trick and dropped a card? Nevertheless, when I was your age, I had an obvious talent for magic. You know, levitating erasers around the classroom when the teacher's back is turned, making spitballs hit their targets around corners, that sort of thing. Eventually I was noticed. I was sent to a special academy in Britain—"

For just an instant, Edward forgot everything that was happening and said, "Wow! Does that mean you knew—?"

"No," his father said, shaking his head and laughing a little. "He was later. But I might have had some of the same teachers."

"Oh."

THE DRAGON HOUSE | 159

"More to the point Edward, I continued playing games with spitballs and erasers, didn't apply myself, and I flunked out. I was still somewhat magical, so eventually I was transferred to the Agency and told in no uncertain terms to shape up or else. I never got to be what perhaps I might have been, but they have me special training, and eventually assigned me to guard the sleeping Dragon House and help raise the next Avatar. That much they thought me capable of, with a certain amount of supervision. They probably made a mistake. They should have gotten somebody else."

Now Edward slid his feet down through the floor again, and felt the strength of the Dragon.

"That's all…very…interesting…" he said in a cold, distant voice. "Is there anything else? Am I in for more surprises?"

"Edward," said Doctor Basileus, "you will lead a long and strange life. You will have many adventures. There will be a lot of surprises. You have to learn to deal with them."

Mom looked at Dad and Dad looked back. "There's one more thing," Mom said. To Dad she said, "We'd better tell him."

Edward said, almost too softly for anyone to hear, "Yes, tell him."

"We're going to have to move away, back to Philadelphia," Dad said. "We, the family, but not you. You stay here. Oh, you could come and visit, but I think that after a while you won't want to. You're the Avatar, remember? We'll just have to visit you. It won't be so bad. It'll be like you've gone away to school."

"Only I don't have the option of flunking out, do I?"

"No."

Now Edward lost control altogether, and just put his head down on his arms on top of the tabletop and sobbed. He didn't feel like an Avatar now, or any kind of hero. He just felt lost, betrayed, hit by so many surprises at once that he'd been pummelled to a pulp.

His mother came over and put her arms around him.

"Now, don't be like that."

He shook her off.

"Go away then! Move away! See if I care!"

"Edward," Dad said softly. "Please don't be angry. Please. I'm begging you, please, don't. Try to understand. Try, even, to forgive. I am sorry, but there are rules about these things. It's for your sister's sake that we have to move away. The house is awake now. It has its Avatar. Magical things will happen. *But she's not magical.* The Dragon House might travel in time or go to other planets. What kind of life would that be for her?"

"I would further point out, Edward," Doctor Basileus, "that time does not move the same inside the house as it does in the rest of the world. I think you have some inkling of that. The Avatar does not age normally. Your sister is two years older than you, but when she is thirty, a grown woman, you might still seem to be fifteen. You could conceivably live for centuries. And when your physical body dies, you will go on, inside the house, like Miss Emily, and *her* many predecessors, whom you will eventually meet. There are parts of what you are, Edward, things you must embrace, which you cannot share, even with your family."

After that, nobody else had anything to say, until Dad suddenly said, "Oh, I almost forgot."

He placed a package on the table in front of Edward.

"What's this?"

"It's almost your birthday, Son. You'll be fourteen in a few days, so I thought you should have this now."

Edward unwrapped it. It was a new laptop computer.

"You wanted your own. Now you won't have to go to the library or share with your sister. You can keep in touch with us that way, all the time. And you can be certain that your wireless internet bills are paid, forever. You'll never have to worry about that."

"Yeah, thanks Dad."

Then everybody else got up and left the room, except for Margaret.

When they were alone, she said, "We'll still visit."

"Uh-huh."

"Now Edward!" she said firmly. She got up. She took hold of him by both shoulders. "Stand up. Get out of that chair."

He stood up. She held on to him.

"Look at me," she said.

He looked.

"I am still your sister, so I can give you some sisterly advice. You're still you. You know it. Stop pretending you're not. That's all that matters."

"Okay," he said softly.

Then she leaned down, touched her forehead to his and whispered something as if it were a deep, dark secret. "Your hair's a mess," she said. "Sometime in the future you're going to discover *girls*, not big sister, but *girls*, and when you do…" She stepped forward playfully onto the hem of his sorcerer's gown and pinned his toes to the floor. "…when you do, you'll find that girls don't necessarily go for boys with messy hair and dirty feet."

He wanted to protest that he was actually quite clean right now, after the epic bath he'd taken, but instead he only smiled at her a little and said, *"Moo…"*

She replied, *"Moo…"* and they both laughed, and he knew, deep in his heart and forever, that "Moo" would always be their private, special greeting, the secret password that linked their lives together, no matter what else happened.

Then she left the room, and he stood there, looking at the computer on the table top. A few minutes ago, he'd felt the impulse to throw it on the floor and smash it in rage, but now he didn't feel any rage. It had all drained away.

After a while he sat down again, and picked up the computer, and held it against his chest, and remained sitting there, in silence, for a long time.

* * * *

For several days thereafter, no one seemed willing to admit they'd said what they had said. Everyone was in denial, even Edward. He thought only to live from moment to moment, not to think about the future.

They had meals as usual. Dad did card tricks in the evenings, without dropping any cards. Margaret helped him get his new computer working. There was even another family picnic in the woods, where nothing in particular happened. They sat under the trees, eating sandwiches, amid awkward silences.

Sometimes he took his sister exploring, into rooms neither one of them has seen before, sometimes back to rooms they had, like the carousel room, which turned when Edward stepped into it, but did nothing if Margaret happened to enter first. There were even doors that would open for him, not for her.

They explored the library, paging through fantastic books. Some of them, too, would not open for her, but fell open at his touch.

He showed her the train layout, which somehow had become even more elaborate than before.

"Was that castle there before?" she asked. "The one with the eyes?"

"I don't think so."

He ran the trains, but when she took the controls, they didn't work.

It wasn't just the days passing by and the leaves on the trees beginning to turn autumn colors that told them that it was time for the rest of the family to let go and move on. The house itself seemed to have gotten the idea.

Then there was the time when he told her to change into a bathing suit and she was to smart to ask if they were going swimming, because she knew that wasn't what he had in mind at all. He'd put on the dragon-hide loincloth, and he took her hand in his and then let himself drop down, through the floor, desperately wishing, hoping that he could pull her through with him, in to the world he so very much wanted to share.

But he should have known better. He *did* know better. Sometimes you just don't want to admit what you really know.

It was like the time he got stuck on his belt-buckle, only worse. He was left dangling in the warm, red, comforting abyss of the dragon's bloodstream, but he could not pull even her hand into the woodwork.

When he finally released his grip he drifted down, down, feeling the conscious presence of the Dragon, but the Dragon did not speak, as if it too realized that this was something Edward would have to learn on his own.

When he finally emerged into his bedroom and changed, and went to meet Margaret, she had already switched back to her everyday clothes and said nothing about what had happened.

There was an afternoon of gunnery practice. They shot the tops off a few trees.

But when they were done, Doctor Basileus was standing in the doorway, with a lesson for Edward to study, all neatly written out on papyrus scrolls and carried in something like a large leather hatbox.

Doctor Basileus nodded to Margaret, silently.

* * * *

A few days later, the family moved away. First a team of gargoyles had to lift the SUV out of the ditch into which it had fallen, down among the trees. Then Dad had to call in a very ordinary contractor to fill in a big gap in the driveway, which he explained had been damaged in the recent "earthquake," the same one about which there were fantastic things printed in the supermarket tabloids, all sorts of nonsense about houses disappearing and whole mountaintops crawling away as if they were alive.

Then there were more goodbyes.

"See you later," said Margaret to Edward. She took him aside and whispered, *"Moo..."*

"Moo," he whispered back.

Edward stood, barefoot and in his sorcerer's robe, watching the SUV disappear down the driveway, into the woods. Then he turned back into the house.

"Master, the doctor is upstairs, waiting to begin today's lesson," said the gargoyle doorman.

"Thanks, Gargy."

"Not Gargy... Oh, very good, sir."

His days and nights were filled after that. He was alone when he wanted to be, but never truly alone, for the House was there, and he was a part of the House and of the Dragon. He swam inside the walls whenever he felt like it, wearing the strip of dragon-hide Miss Emily had given him, though he didn't need the knife anymore and left it in a drawer.

Inside, he had long talks with Miss Emily, and she introduced him to Josiah Willet, who had been master of the Dragon House in 1750, and to Sky Serpent Walking, an Iroquois shaman, who had known a very different Dragon House in the 16th century.

The Agency made sure he was well supplied with tutors and guardians, most often Doctor Basileus, who took up residence in one of the towers, and Zarcon of Zarconax, but there were many more, not to mention a considerable supply of minions.

He studied hard. He learned new and amazing things. He spent many hours in the library, which the Librarian and his (or its) assistants had somehow restored to impeccable neatness.

Edward was in touch with Margaret on the e-mail almost every night. Sometimes he sent her photos he'd taken of magical realms, or views from other planets.

He did occasionally lose track of time, and so he was caught by surprise one snowy, winter afternoon.

He had finished his formal lessons for the day, and was lying on a couch in the living room, reading. He hadn't been able to concentrate on Henry Armitage's *Necronomicon for Beginners* and so had turned to his latest favorite, *The Adventures of Sherlock Holmes,* trying to imagine a fantastic world where things worked by logic and natural laws, where physical objects could be relied upon to remain as they appeared, and the rooms in houses didn't change their configurations overnight.

He heard the doorbell ring, and put the book down, but didn't get up.

"You may go in," said the gargoyle doorman. "I am sure the Master will be pleased to see you."

Then Margaret was in the room, holding an armload of packages, some of which she dropped as she put one hand to her mouth to prevent herself from laughing when she saw how he was dressed: his dragon-embroidered robe open at the front like a bath robe, over sweatshirt and sweat pants, then bright red and white striped socks, and a soft, floppy, stovepipe sort of hat pulled down around his ears, red and white striped to match the socks. And he was wearing the bunny-rabbit slippers.

Then Dad came in, took one look, and said, "You know Son, you have the makings of a really first-rate eccentric. But that's fine. That's good."

Edward sat up. He didn't quite know what to say.

Mom came in, with more packages.

"Have you forgotten, Edward? It's Christmas!"

"We brought a tree," Dad said. "It's in the car."

"I could have made the house grow a tree," Edward said. "But it's more fun to set it up and decorate it ourselves, don't you think?"

"Aren't you going to say hello?" said Mom.

"Hello."

"HELLO EDWARD! MERRY CHRISTMAS EDWARD!" everyone else said at once.

He could have had the gargoyles do the work, but instead he took off the slippers and put on ordinary rubber boots that he kept in the closet by the door, and waded out in the snow to help them unload the tree and the ornaments and their suitcases and much else.

He hadn't forgotten Christmas entirely. He had another closet full of presents for them upstairs.

They put up the tree and decorated it. They had to move a few things, because the living room was getting a bit cluttered, its latest decor including a stuffed bear reared up on its hind legs, a life-sized statue of a samurai, and an enormous, two-headed tortoise made of stone. But they found a way.

Mom cooked a fine Christmas dinner, complete with one of her special pies, and afterwards they all sat around the tree by the fireplace and unwrapped presents, and for the moment at least, however oddly time might drift inside the Dragon House, or whatever strangeness awaited in the future, everything was fine, because they were together and they were a family.

Made in the USA
Middletown, DE
04 November 2022